KILLERS IN THE RAIN

I crossed the square to Donegall Place, bending into the slanting rain, hoping to lose the pale man in the crowds of rain-soaked shoppers. I turned around and saw a second man in a doorway behind me. He was bigger, with thinning gray hair, wearing a ski jacket and jeans. I decided I'd rather deal with the smaller man. I walked straight at him, through the bustle of the crowd, spit in his face, and kept going.

He came after me. I turned left at the corner, then right again on an empty street lined with fire-gutted buildings. And waited. I heard footsteps. Then suddenly he was there, turning the corner, his eyes wide in alarm. I hit him with a right hand that jolted my shoulder when it landed. He went down in the rain without saying a word.

The second one wasn't so easy.

Golden Apple Books by Pete Hamill

THE DEADLY PIECE
DIRTY LAUNDRY

THE GUNS OF HEAVEN

Pete Hamill

A Sam Briscoe Thriller

GOLDEN APPLE PUBLISHERS

THE GUNS OF HEAVEN

A Golden Apple Publication / June 1985

Golden Apple is a trademark of Golden Apple Publishers

ISBN 0-553-19833-5

For my brother Tom
Companion of the Pearl Street Mornings

THE GUNS
OF
HEAVEN

1 It was raining in Belfast when the British Airways Viscount from London slowed for its approach to Aldergrove Airport. The rain, of course, was not unusual. To my mind, it is always raining in Belfast, a fine, sad, steady rain, dirty with the smoke of mills and shipyards and a hundred thousand coal fires glowing in the front-room grates of the squashed row houses. The Belfast rain is dirty with other things, too. Hurting things. Old angers, unforgiven grievances, the ashen taste of death. And the rain never stops.

"Have ye been to Belfast before?" said the Scotsman in the seat beside me. I glanced at his florid face, his dying pipe and tweed jacket, as the plane bumped down on the runway. He looked like a man who could no longer sell what he had sold for years.

"Yes," I said. "It's a tough city."

"Aye," the Scotsman said, "and a sad one, too."

I didn't go on talking. I didn't say that I had been coming to Belfast since 1962, stopping off on my way to or from other places in the world. I didn't say that every time I came back, there was less of Belfast, or less of me. The bombs had leveled old bars where I had sung with relatives and friends in the tight, ageless, steamy world of mahogany and chased mirrors and mugs of dark, creamy Guinness. I didn't tell the Scotsman about the little sailor from Bombay Street, who knew the verses of every Cole Porter song ever written and mixed them with sea chanteys and Irish ballads and laughter one long drunken night in 1965 until we all staggered back to the hotel together and passed out in the lobby; or how Bombay Street had been leveled in the fires of 1969, when the Murder Gang was unleashed by the Orange Order to pour into the streets of the Catholic ghetto,

1

burning, maiming, and destroying; and how, in the morning ashes, the Provisional IRA had been born. The little seaman from Bombay Street was dead five months later, his body found in a country field in Antrim with his throat cut and a note about papist killers pinned to his chest.

I didn't mention him to the Scotsman, nor did I talk about all those other streets of Belfast which had seemed so much like another home to me when I first went there to meet my mother's brother Frank Houlihan: streets where everybody rode bicycles; where old men with cloth caps stood on corners and argued about soccer, or the effect of the Panama Canal on the weather of Ireland; where young girls left school at fourteen to work in the mills, and fell in love with boys who made them gaudy promises of life in America or Australia or London town. Those streets had filled later with Saracen tanks and British troops with thick polished boots, and some of the mill girls learned to assemble Armalite machine guns in thirty-six seconds, while the boys began again to sing ballads about dying for Ireland. Others had left home, joining the endless Irish diaspora; those who stayed were sadder and tougher each time I came back, and after awhile I, too, had come to think of the six northern counties as Occupied Ireland. But I didn't say that to the Scotsman.

"Are you stayin' long?"

"A few days, and then home," I lied. I don't like people who ask too many questions on airplanes.

"Well, try to enjoy it."

"Thanks."

The plane taxied to a stop, and we waited for the doors to open. Safety belts unclicked like the sound of rifles being cocked. Through the rain-streaked window I could see British paratroopers lounging against the wall of the main building, loosely holding machine guns, a few of them smoking furtively. In front of the main gate, six members of the Royal Ulster Constabulary seemed more alert and somehow more British than the paratroopers, standing tall and stiff and implacable, with the February rain running down their dark blue gabardine coats. The doors finally opened, and one of the RUC men came into the plane, planting his broad wet back against the cockpit door, searching the face of each passenger as we filed past him. I was glad that I was not too young or too long-haired or more than half-Irish. I was also glad that I was not packing a gun.

I went past him, carrying my Hermes 3000, and walked down the stairway. The Belfast smell blended with the rain, a compost of burning wax candles from too many churches, wet wool and unwashed feet and cheap cigarettes, cordite and ruined plaster and despair. The smell and the rain reminded me again that I hated coming to Belfast, and I went into the main building past the lolling soldiers to the customs area, feeling tired and dirty.

An Irishman in a British uniform pawed through my one bag, telling me to first open the typewriter and play the tape recorder, then directing me to passport control. A thin young man with watery blue eyes waited for me behind a dais. I handed him my passport. He looked at my photograph and then at me.

"You've lost some hair?"

"Yeah."

"Nature of visit?"

"Business."

"What business?" he said sharply.

"I'm a reporter."

"Yes?"

"I'm doing an article on the, uh, problems here in Northern Ireland."

He blinked, stared carefully at my picture again, as if trying to remember some other photograph, and then stamped an inside page and passed me through.

"Have a good visit to Ulster."

"I'll try."

I walked toward a narrow passageway that led to the outer waiting room and the baggage. I glanced behind me, and saw a large tweedy man with a red moustache speaking to the passport clerk. They were watching me.

2 Frank Houlihan was waiting beside the newsstand, his gaunt pale face leaner than it had ever been. He was wearing a gray raincoat that was almost dry, and he only resembled my mother around the eyes, which were brown and amused. He extended his left hand; the withered right arm, smashed by a British bullet in some forgotten campaign, was stuffed into a pocket of the raincoat.

"Hello, Sam," he said, squeezing my hand and then reaching for the suitcase.

"Hello, Uncle Frank. Hey, I'll take that."

He smiled: "I can still lift a man's load, even if I *am* seventy-two, Sam."

"The only thing I want you lifting is a glass of porter."

"Well, we'll do that, too."

I took the bag away from him, and we moved across the waiting room through a crowd of Irish faces—the young children racing around, the worn, older faces bouncing up and down at the sight of each new arrival, waiting for relatives and friends, and cheering when they saw each other. I changed two hundred dollars into pounds at the Barclay's Bank and bought all the newspapers.

"I never thought I'd see you here again," Frank said. "I'm glad you called."

"Some editor in New York wants his annual St. Patrick's Day piece on the Irish, and I want to see my daughter in Switzerland. So we made a deal. I charged the editor for the trip to Switzerland, with a stop in Ireland first."

Frank smiled, but his voice was sardonic. "I suppose it's just that one bloody day they think of us in America, isn't it?"

"That's about it," I said. "Twenty-four hours of 'Danny Boy' and 'Galway Bay,' and they can forget Ireland for another year."

We stepped out into the rain. A noisy mess of buses,

4

taxis, and cars. Soldiers everywhere. Overpainted graffiti. Rain. Frank led the way between two large red Leyland buses.

"How is wee April, Sam?"

"She's fine, Uncle Frank. It's not easy when you're eleven years old and off on your own. But she's coming along nicely. The worst news is that she's just discovered Dostoyevsky and wants to be a writer."

"*Another* writer?" he laughed.

"I keep telling her to learn something practical, like fixing air-conditioners. But she's got the bug."

Frank waved; a small man with a shriveled-apple face stepped out of a car and came over to grab the bag and the typewriter.

"This it, Frank?" the man said. "Nothing more?"

"Aye, and you know where we're going."

The man darted away, carrying the bags, with the two of us following. Frank said: "I've sent word to yer mon. I let them know y' didn't have much time."

"I hope he can do it."

"He'll be around."

We got into the back of the car, passed two more soldiers in black berets, and drove fast into the countryside. Frank offered me a Woodbine; I took it and he snapped open a throwaway lighter. The tobacco was harsh after the milder American blends.

"Well, how is it here, Uncle Frank?"

"Ach, Sam, it's Belfast, and it's worse than ever."

"I don't see how it could be worse."

"It's the corruption," he said. "The Brits have corrupted everyone. They tried guns, rubber bullets, internment. Nothing worked. They wiretapped all the bloody phones and sealed the bloody border. Nothing worked. Then they brought the money. That worked. They've spread the Queen's shillin' among starvin' men, so there's informers everywhere."

"The oldest Irish story."

"Aye. And the saddest."

We passed a few ruined cottages and piles of burnt

5

bramble, cleared by the British to keep snipers away from touring businessmen. A car rusted in a field. There were black clouds in the mountains.

"There's been some disciplinary action lately," Frank said quietly. "That's never nice. Nobody likes to shoot a former comrade."

I moved my eyes from Frank to the driver.

"He's all right," Frank said, and took a heavy drag on the Woodbine. "He's all right."

Frank would certainly know. He was an old man now, but he had been fighting this war since he was thirteen. He knew the real soldiers. And he knew the Saturday night patriots, the singers of brave ballads who always vanished one fine morning, a step ahead of the Special Branch. I had seen a lot of those men myself, singing their endless death-ridden ballads in the safe bars of America; Irish songs, I thought then, were the last refuge of scoundrels.

But Frank Houlihan was a serious man. He didn't fight his war with songs. He fired his first rifle for the IRA in the Civil War that followed the 1921 treaty which divided Ireland into a twenty-six-county republic in the South and a six-county British colony in the North. He was on the side of the men who said that a divided Ireland would never be at peace. Those men were right, and Frank had given his life to them. He had served time in British prisons; had seen his children, growing up as strangers, depart for England and Australia as soon as they were old enough to leave; saw his wife wither young, poisoned by the death around her, dying herself in grateful acceptance; had seen comrades die, betray themselves and each other, or sicken with despair; and Frank Houlihan soldiered on.

He would write to my mother from prison camps in England and wish her a good life in America; he wrote about the honor of death when my father was killed trying to stop a holdup, his detective's badge an inch from the bullet; he wrote that he would see her again some day, as they walked the streets of a free Belfast, with the tricolor flying on all the rooftops of a united Ireland. But she died without ever seeing him again, and I met him for the first time when

I took her body home, to be returned to the Irish earth. The North was quiet that year, but late one night, I asked Frank Houlihan if the old struggle for a united Ireland was over, and he looked at me in a chilling way and said: "It's never over." And he was, of course, right. A lot of things are never over.

"Will y' be wantin' to see your mother?" he asked, as the driver slowed in the first cobbled streets of Belfast.

"No, Frank. I'm no good at prayers. Or graveyards."

"Fair enough."

He was quiet for a long moment. Then: "It's good to see you, Sam."

"I feel the same about you, Uncle Frank."

"I know that," he said, his voice quick with the clipped Belfast burr.

"It doesn't seem like fifteen years since all of this started," I said.

He laughed in a dry way. "Fifteen years? It's more like eight hundred, lad."

We were in the outskirts of the city now, and the weather-stained brick walls were covered with the foot-high graffiti of civil war. REBELS BEWARE and NO IRA HERE and FUCK THE POPE. We were in the Shankill, the heart of the Protestant section. Union Jacks flapped in the wet wind. We stopped for a red light, and saw three men standing together in the doorway of a horse parlor. One of them looked up from his Belfast *News-Letter*, and stared at us. The others tensed. Frank leaned back in the car, out of their vision, the reflex action of a man who had lived his life in the shadows of history. The light turned green and we moved away from them.

"I wish sometimes I could get out and talk to them and tell them we're not their enemies," Frank said quietly. "Just tell them how the fuckers in the big houses have kept us apart for three hundred years, killing and fighting and cursing each other. Now's the time to end it all. Now's the time to make Ireland one country again and get rid of the bloody past."

"Have you ever tried to talk to them?"

"No." He lit a second Woodbine from the stump of the first. "But I've thought about it."

"Maybe some of them have, too."

"Aye, that's possible. But the way things are goin', we might never find out."

The car slowed. There was an army barricade at the next corner. Ahead of us, five cars waited patiently on line. We were on a street of small two-story houses. On the roof to our right a British soldier leaned against a chimney, a machine gun in his hand, watching the cars. There were two Saracen tanks behind the barricade, one with its cannon pointing in the direction of the Catholic section, the other at the Protestants. Three soldiers in black berets huddled in a cube of sandbags. More sandbags, topped with rolls of barbed wire, blocked the street, allowing space for only one car to pass. More cars were waiting on the other side of the bags. I was carrying no guns, but as we came to the search-point, my stomach tightened. A soldier with rolled-up sleeves, his hand on the trigger of a machine gun, came over to the driver's side and peered in. His face was pink and very young.

"What business have ye in Belfast?"

"I'm carrying an American reporter," the driver said. "To the Europa Hotel."

That was a lie; I was going to the International Hotel. The soldier looked at me, and then at Frank. I could see nothing in his eyes.

"Out," he said.

We stepped out, and the door of one of the small houses opened. A short wiry lieutenant marched briskly toward us, his polished paratrooper boots clacking on the cobblestones. Frank took a lazy drag on the Woodbine, and gazed at the man on the rooftop. I shoved my hands into my pockets and leaned against the fender of the car.

"Papers, please!" the lieutenant snapped. I handed him my passport; he looked at the photograph and then at me. He also leafed through the visas in the passport, rubber-stamped souvenirs of an assortment of countries where people had killed each other in wars. Behind us, cars were lined all the way up the hill. The lieutenant handed me the passport. Then he looked at Frank.

"What are you doing with this scum?" he said to me, his eyes on Frank.

"This scum is my uncle."

He looked at me and then at Frank: "I don't see any resemblance at all."

"You don't look much like Queen Victoria, either, lieutenant."

That was clearly a mistake. The lieutenant's mouth twisted.

"Turn it over," he snapped to the younger soldier, and then stepped back, with some clicking of his heels. The young soldier sighed.

"I'm a British object, said the Belfast man," I said to Frank.

"That's not very funny."

"It was funnier when Brendan Behan said it. You had to be there."

"You are there, Sam."

The first soldier nudged me with the machine gun, and the three of us spread our palms flat out on the black metal sides of the taxi, while a second soldier patted us down. The lieutenant watched in silence. When they finished searching us, they made the driver open the hood and the trunk. One of the soldiers lifted out my suitcase and the typewriter, and told me to open them. I was obviously not hiding a mortar in the typewriter, but the suitcase was more interesting to them. The lieutenant came over to see what I was carrying. A book was lying on top of my bathrobe.

"Stendhal?" he said. "*On Love*?" He snickered. "Amusing."

"It is," I said. "You should read it."

"It's the wrong country for that subject."

One of the soldiers was tossing my clothes around, while two others searched under the seats of the car.

"All right, let them through," the lieutenant said. My bag lay open, the clothes rumpled and disturbed.

"Just a minute, lieutenant," I said. "You haven't finished."

He blinked, his blond eyelashes fluttering.

"You've got to pack my clothes," I said.

"What?"

"I said you have to fold the clothing," I said. "I already went through customs at the airport. I came here, as an American citizen on legitimate business, and my clothes were neatly folded. They are not folded now. I want them folded, pal."

His eyes turned the color of slush. "Pal?"

"Yeah."

His hand rested on the pistol. "You called me 'pal?'"

"Is the word on the proscribed list?"

Two of the soldiers inched back, as if for firing room. The slushy eyes slowly focused, and the lieutenant gave me a wintry smile. Then he turned on his heel and said to the pink-faced soldiers: "Fold them."

I could hear Frank Houlihan release a breath.

3 The International is a "Catholic" hotel. Part of the lunacy of Belfast is that such a distinction remains possible in the last fifth of the twentieth century. With a nod to the desk clerk, Frank took me directly to my room and then went off, promising to be back in three hours.

The room was spare, almost monastic: a narrow celibate bed, a small glass-topped table, a bureau, a door leading to the bathroom. I put the typewriter on the table, washed up, and then started to type while I waited.

I was waiting for a man named Commander Steel. In the previous year he had emerged as one of the most important, and shadowy, leaders of the Provisional IRA. I had heard of him in New York, but only about his role; nothing of his life. Nobody knew his full name. Nobody knew what he looked like. But in this latest phase of IRA warfare, the various local commands had been restructured into small four-man cells, to prevent infiltration and isolate informers. Discipline was infinitely better, targets were more precise, weapons more effective, and the overall strategy was apparently directed by Commander Steel. When I first heard the name, talking to a friendly bartender, I laughed out loud. He sounded like a character out of a comic book. But when I asked about him in IRA circles in New York, men nodded, and said, aye, he's the one. A few claimed that he had served in the British Army in Cyprus and Malaya, and was a superb strategist because he could anticipate all of the British moves. Others claimed that in the 1960's he had served as a Green Beret with the Americans during the early years of the Vietnam war. Whatever his background, the latest IRA offensive had been devastating and deadly. In separate operations on a single day, they had killed Earl Mountbatten and eighteen members of the Second Paratroop Battalion, the largest number of British soldiers killed in one engagement in Ireland since the IRA was formed. Before that, within a few months, they had killed one British cabinet minister, two colonels, and sixteen infantrymen. They had destroyed eleven major factories, in the continuing campaign to neutralize industry in the North, and they had blown the Dublin-Belfast train off its tracks. With the exception of the passengers on Mountbatten's boat, no innocent people had been killed. In the early days, that had not been true. The early Provos were overly fond of gelignite, an explosive as unstable as the Irish weather. Sometimes, when a driver hit a bump in a road, the gelignite blew up the car on the way to a target, killing passersby and the deadly messengers themselves.

Sometimes a bomb went off early, before warnings could be called into the newspapers or the RUC, and television would show the bodies of children. It was a disgusting time. There were other times, during one long ugly phase, when the Special Branch chose to ignore warnings and let the bombs go off, killing or maiming civilians, so that the IRA would be discredited among Catholics and in the American press. All of that now seemed to be in the past.

Now someone was choosing solid targets. Execution had been near-flawless. And in certain New York bars, where such things are always known, it was said that the planning was done by a man named Steel. When I knew that I would be coming to Ireland, I sent a note to Frank Houlihan, asking him to set up an interview with Steel. Three days later, the Aer Lingus stewardess who had delivered the note met me in P. J. Clarke's and told me that my uncle Frank had a simple message for me: "I'll try."

And so I was waiting in this monk-like shabby room in a second-rate hotel for a man I'd never met. I couldn't afford to sleep; if I did, I'd go under with jet lag and exhaustion. I had to go out and breathe some air. I went into the small bathroom, washed my hands and face, pulled on a tweed jacket and went out to look at the sad, wounded city.

The rain was still falling steadily. I went into a clothing store in the next block and bought an umbrella. And when I stepped out of the shop and opened the umbrella, I picked up the tail. He was a pale thin man in a wrinkled navy blue suit, and he was across the street staring into a window display of antique marine paintings. He was alone.

I walked down the street to Donegall Square, where a hideous statue of Queen Victoria squatted in seedy splendor in front of the City Hall. The Queen had visited the city in 1849, and her grim, joyless visage had glowered bitterly at the inhabitants ever since. I pretended to look up at the facade of the City Hall, its Portland stone, mock-Renaissance bulk stained by time and the rain. The tail stared off at a group of sculpted figures on the east side of the building. I knew from other visits that those figures were part of the only monument anywhere in the world dedicated to the victims of the Titanic, which had been built in Belfast. The setting, of course, was perfect.

I crossed the square to Donegall Place, bending into the slanting rain, hoping to lose the pale man in the crowds of rain-soaked shoppers. The massive Palladian columns of the department stores rose above us, monuments to imperial optimism, their lower windows now boarded over or bricked up, while a million starlings huddled on their edges. There were no cars parked on the street; they had been banned during the days of the car bombings and had never come back. An army patrol marched by in the rain, but none of the Irish bothered to look. I ducked into a department store, quickly folding the umbrella, hurried through counters piled with pink silky mounds of underwear, and went out another door. Then I glanced behind me but couldn't see the pale man. I crossed one of the side streets, walking quickly through the crowds, but not so quickly that I'd look like a bomber. I stole glances of my own reflection in the windows, but the tail was gone.

And then he was up ahead, standing in the doorway of a betting parlor, smoking a cigarette, never looking at me.

I turned around and saw a second man in a doorway behind me. He was bigger, with thinning gray hair, wearing a ski jacket and jeans. I decided I'd rather deal with the smaller man. I walked straight at him, through the bustle of the crowd, spit in his face, and kept going.

He came after me. I carried the folded umbrella like a spear, cut to the right down a side street, turned left at the corner, then right again on an empty street lined with fire-gutted buildings. And waited. The rain poured down now. I thought of stabbing him with the umbrella, but the idea repelled me. I heard footsteps. Then suddenly he was there, turning the corner, his eyes wide in alarm. I hit him with a right hand that jolted my shoulder when it landed. He went down in the rain without saying a word.

The second one wasn't so easy. As I was looking down at the small pale man, feeling like Rocky Marciano, the big man turned the corner, a pistol jammed in his belt.

I lunged for the gun, but he whacked me on the upper arm, grabbed my coat front, whirled me around like I was a sack of coffee beans, slamming me against the wall. Jesus Christ. He held me there, as if ready to punish me. I lifted a knee into his balls, and he backed up.

"For Christ's sake, mon," he hissed, "we're tryin' to *protect* you!"

"You're here to protect me?" I said, feeling as foolish as he looked.

"You're in Belfast, mon," he said. "The other side has people everywhere. On Donegall Street alone, the Brits've got a hundred whores who'd take the Queen's shillin'. They'd like nothin' better than a Yank reporter with his throat cut, and a fake letter from the Provos pinned to his chest."

He reached down for the other man. "Now, give us a hand with this poor booger, before the fookin' Brits see us."

I believed him. I had no choice. I knew that there were killers everywhere; I also knew that among the irregular infantry of the "other side" there were a lot of men who would kill me gladly. Psy-war, they called it in Saigon in the old days. You killed people and blamed the other side and sat back to read the outraged editorials that were certain to follow. Such things had been going on in Belfast since 1969; they were part of the brutal terrain.

"Did Steel tell you to watch me?" I said.

He gave me a look, but said nothing. That was like saying everything. I helped him lift the little man out of the gutter and into the hallway of an abandoned building. The hall smelled of things wet and dead. The big man shoved me down, and then through the cracked door we could see a Saracen tank rumble by. The smaller man groaned. When I couldn't hear the Saracen anymore I stood up.

"Tell Steel I'm waiting to see him," I said, and went back out into the rain. My back ached. I was very tired. I picked up my umbrella and returned to the hotel.

Back in the room, I took the doilies off the glass-topped table to keep the typewriter from moving around, and started writing again what is called in the trade, B-copy. I hated writing B-copy because it always smelled of the clips; B-copy was what you wrote while the famous movie actor was undergoing his third stomach operation; you wrote all the highlights of his life, while waiting for the final highlight, after which you would never use the clips again.

You put the fresh news at the top, and filled in the story with all the old news.

So I was writing old news, even sketching the long and turbulent history of the North of Ireland, from the arrival of Strongbow's English armies in 1157 to the present, and waiting for Frank Houlihan to put me together with Steel. Steel was fresh news, but the agony of Ireland was the oldest news of all.

Someone knocked at the door. I asked who it was.

"A pot of tea, sir?"

I opened the door and a pasty little waiter stood there, holding a tray of standard room service items: a pot, a cup and saucer, a pitcher of milk, and some buttered bread. In the Catholic hotel, you apparently got room service whether you ordered it or not.

"Great," I said. "Come in."

Then someone moved from the side, and I was shoved back inside the room, falling to a sitting position on the small bed. I looked up at a medium-sized man in his thirties. He had a helmet of gray curly hair, his complexion the color of tallow. His cheeks were rough with old acne, and tufts of black hair protruded from his nose. He would have been ugly if it weren't for his eyes. They were an icy emerald green, oddly feminine, and they dominated his face. The eyes were wide and wary as he came in, and then when the waiter politely closed the door, they narrowed to a chilly squint. He stared at me, rubbing his blue unshaven chin with his right hand. In his left hand he was holding a .38-caliber Smith and Wesson revolver.

"Who the hell *are* you, mate?" he said.

I got up slowly from the bed, trying to ignore the gun. As I rose, the gun hand rose, the deadly little hole pointed at my chest. "You know who I am," I said. "My name is Briscoe. Sam Briscoe. I'm an American. A reporter. I'm writing an article on the war here."

"You've got proof of this?" the man said. His voice was deep and hoarse, as if its upper registers had been wire-brushed away.

"My passport's on top of the bureau," I said. "My

wallet has my New York City press card in it. Help yourself. But you don't really need that fucking gun."

The green eyes got colder as he lowered the gun and edged over to the bureau. The waiter was still standing next to the closed door with his tray of tea and bread. The man with the gun looked at my passport, and a nerve twitched in his pitted face.

"Bring us another pot of tea, Pat," the man said. The waiter put the tray down on the bed. "And for Christ's sake, make it hot."

"Yes, sir," Pat said, and went out, closing the door behind him. Almost delicately, the man with the green eyes inserted the gun into a holster on his ankle. The only sound was the wet Belfast wind bumping against the window. His eyes examined me from behind the mask of ugliness.

"Hello," he said. "I'm Steel."

4 He smiled thinly when he congratulated me for taking out one of the men who was supposed to be protecting me. He told me how much he loved my Uncle Frank. Then we talked through seven pots of tea and two packs of Woodbines. First, he gave me *his* B-copy, talking for the tape recorder, tracing the history of Ulster from the Plantation under Elizabeth I to the founding of the Provisional IRA. He spoke of the Battle of the Boyne as if it had happened last year, not in 1689; he talked bitterly about the Plantation, the move by Elizabeth I and her successors to plant loyal Protestants in the North of Ireland, thus insuring that Catholic France and Catholic Spain would have no friendly real estate from which to invade the underbelly of England. He reminded me that the native Irish in the North had been removed from all of the good farmland and forced to scrape a dismal living from the rocky hills, or to emigrate. He said a lot of things that I already knew.

"The Israelis are making the same mistake now that England made then," he said, his voice oddly soft.

"They're planting settlers in the occupied territory of the West Bank, in the name of 'security.' Three hundred years from now, the Palestinians will still be fighting them there."

Then he sketched the various historical shifts among the Protestants: the way the Presbyterians grew increasingly liberal in Ireland, chafing under the snobbery and the power of the Anglican Church, the official church of England. The Irish Presbyterians, by the end of the eighteenth century, had begun to see themselves as Irishmen first, Protestants second, and Wolfe Tone, a Protestant, became the leader of the Irish Revolution of 1798. I soon realized that Steel saw me only as a platform upon which he could stand and speak. Fair enough, as Frank Houlihan would say. Some men did things, other men listened. Most of the time I listened.

"Tone said he was on the side of the men of no property," he said. "For awhile the Protestant artisans and shopkeepers listened, then the English divided them again with religion. When the 1798 rebellion failed, and Tone died, the English panicked. They decided to revive the prostrate Catholic Church. They built the seminary in Maynooth, outside Dublin, and imported a load of French Jansenists—on the lam, as you Americans say, from the French Revolution—and let them run it. They ran it, all right: for their English sponsors. The Church was on the side of the powerful for the next two hundred years, clamping its dead hands on the neck of the Irish character. We were—and are—a people of passion, of volcanic feeling; but they strangled us with their gray little hands. No wonder we've so often looked like a nation of drunks and gunmen."

I let him talk, and watched him carefully, particularly his hands. He was clearly no man of the bogs; the words came in paragraphs, the grammar scanned. And his hands were not the hands of a mill worker. The fingers were long and tapered, and the nails gleamed. He used them to underline his points, as if they could provide italics or capitals, or even a sound track.

"Ever since, the English have used religion to divide

the Catholic working class from the Protestant working class," he went on. "Unlike England, there was never a viable labor movement here, or a viable socialist party. It was like your American South, where blacks and whites were separated by the ludicrous accident of color. The result? In the North of Ireland, ninety-five percent of the land is owned by five percent of the people. That five percent got rich by being part of the British Empire. Now the Empire is gone, and they're holding on. They're fools, of course, But they are murderous fools, so we must fight."

"Are you a socialist?"

"Yes. And that's why the Republic isn't interested in us. They're running a bloody real estate company down there, not a government. Selling Ireland to the highest bidders—Germans, Japanese, Americans. Ireland for sale. We socialists will stop all that, even reverse it. That's why they don't want any part of us."

His accent was Irish, but there was a peculiar American rhythm to his words.

"When did you leave the States?" I said.

He seemed surprised. "I didn't say I'd ever lived anywhere but Belfast."

"But you have."

He stared at me. "Yes."

"Tell me about it."

"I don't think so."

"Then tell me about yourself. Tell me what it's like to be a leader of the Provos."

"I don't matter."

"Bullshit."

"I'm not a leader," he said, his voice curling into bitterness. "We've had enough fucking leaders."

"Every revolution has leaders."

"Yes," he said, "and they ride around on their fucking white horses, and then someone comes along and shoots them off their white horses, and they carry their movements to the grave. I'm just a soldier. One of many."

I lit a Woodbine and sipped the sweet tea. "How do I know you are who you say you are?"

"You don't."

"That's exactly what I mean," I said. "You could be anyone. Nobody's even seen this Commander Steel. You could be from Actor's Equity, or the British Special Branch, for that matter. You could tell me almost anything and I might have to write it down and put it in print, because I'm on such a tight goddamned deadline. You could tell me all that generalized historical bullshit and never have to tell me anything specific. Chances are you won't tell me who the hell Steel is because you aren't Steel. You just don't know."

He took out a solid handkerchief and blew his nose with a loud, almost vulgar honking sound. He smiled: "Well, if I were a Catholic, I'd tell you, Briscoe, that there are some things that must be accepted on faith alone."

"You're not a Catholic?"

"I believe in Ireland."

"So did Wolfe Tone," I said. "And he was a Protestant."

"Aye," he said, making clear that such a conversation was not going to be part of the interview. Then he checked his watch, one of those digital jobs with an American brand name made by the Japanese.

"Do you need anything else?" he said, abruptly.

"Yeah. A guide. Someone to drive me through Andersonstown and New Lodge Road and down to the Shankill. Someone who knows his way around, particularly after dark."

"He's in the lobby," Steel said flatly. "There isn't much to see."

"I know."

He stood up, and pulled a drag on the cigarette.

"I must be off," he said, but he didn't move.

"I wish you'd tell me something about yourself," I said quietly. "It's not going to be very believable otherwise."

He eased his tapered hands into his pockets. The left hand fondled the gun. "You write for the magazine section of a newspaper that is written for an elite, by an elite. In that section, you tell people how to find psychiatrists and private

19

schools and the best rye bread. You think *I* should be believable?"

I laughed out loud. The description of the newspaper's feature section was absolutely accurate.

"Okay, you're right," I said. "But those elites have a certain amount of power. The British propaganda people would never ignore them. I don't think you can afford to ignore them either."

He chewed the inside of his lip. And then he seemed to make a decision.

"What do you want to know?"

"About you."

"What about me?" he said.

"Who are you? Where do you come from? Do you have a wife? Do—"

"I had a wife."

"Where is she now?"

"She was coming home one night from a concert in the Albert Hall," he said. "She was with my son Michael. Three cars cut them off. Six men in ski masks came out of the cars with machine pistols. UVF—"

"The Ulster Volunteer Force—"

"Aye. The stupidest crowd of all the loyalist paramilitary outfits. And the most murderous. They bundled Moira and Michael into the cars and drove off into the night. When they didn't come home, I called a friend and we drove around looking for them all over Belfast."

"And?"

"We found the bodies two days later in the hills beyond the lough," he said. "It was a beautiful summer day. The grass was never greener. The lake was like glass." He exhaled. "Moira had her throat cut. There were knife wounds all over her breasts. Michael had a bullet hole in his back. They'd cut his penis off." His voice was flat as tin now. "We never found it. I suppose one of the fuckers collects them."

"Jesus Christ."

"Jesus Christ had nothing to do with it," he said, looking directly at me. "Except in the most general way."

I felt as if I had done something dirty, getting him to tell the story, even in its abbreviated form.

"Why them?" I said. "If you're IRA, that's one thing. But the—"

"I wasn't even IRA," he said. "I was in the civil rights movement then. Out at the university. I believed in sweet reason, in pacifism, in Gandhi and Martin Luther King, and turn the other cheek."

"But why—?"

"They didn't believe us," he said. "The bloody loyalists had been taught for fifty years that every criticism of the Ulster government was part of an IRA plot. At the time, I didn't know a single IRA man. But since I was a Protestant, they wanted to believe I'd gone over to the IRA, the worst kind of turncoat. They were wrong. I just wanted justice for everybody. A bloody idealist. And they killed my wife and son because of it."

"What did you do?"

"I went away. I was in Amsterdam and Paris for a few months and then went to New York. I changed my name a dozen times. I thought I could get rid of the past and my hatred by becoming someone else. I was gone three years. But the hatred didn't go away and neither did the war. I came home and joined the Provisional IRA."

"For revenge?"

"At first. But then I realized that there could be no end to revenge. I'd have to kill too many people. I want the war to end. I want the killing to stop, once and forever."

"But you're still killing people."

"The right people," he said bitterly. "At last."

I asked him about the Green Berets, and whether he had ever been in the British Army, but he wouldn't talk about either story. He seemed tired and sour, the green eyes avoiding contact with mine.

"A few more big operations," he said, "and it'll end. The British public won't stand for much more of this."

"You believe that?"

"Yes."

21

He crushed a cigarette into the overflowing ashtray. I turned off the tape recorder.

"I'm sorry," I said.

"For what?"

"For asking you to dredge up all that pain."

"Sorrow is a disease," he said wearily. "There's no cure for it. All you can do is fight. Just fight on. And on. And on."

I hit the reject button on the tape recorder and the cassette popped out, and I tucked it into a nylon slot on the side of my suitcase. He lit another cigarette.

"Now I have a favor to ask from you," he said.

"What is it?"

"I need a letter delivered to a place in New York," he said. "In Queens. It's important."

I looked at him for a beat. The long slender hands were kneading each other. He didn't seem like a revolutionary hero, a legendary figure, nor a cold-blooded killer. He was just a man who believed in an abstraction called Ireland, and had gone down a road that very few human beings would ever have to choose: the road of the hunted, the road of the emotionally marooned, the road of the believer.

"I don't know," I said. "This isn't my war."

"I understand."

He took a letter from inside his tweed jacket, and hefted it. On the plain white envelope, I could see a typed name and address in Queens, in the city of New York.

"Why should you trust me?" I said. "What makes you think I wouldn't take that letter and run its contents on page one of a newspaper?"

"Your uncle Frank bought my trust," he said. "With all the years of his life. If it were not for men like him, I wouldn't be here."

"Does he know about this?"

"Yes."

"And he told you I'd do it?"

"No, he gave me permission to ask you."

I lit a cigarette. "That's the only reason you asked me to play messenger boy?"

"No."

The cigarette tasted sour. He stared at me. The emerald eyes didn't blink.

"I liked the way you handled my men," he said. A smile started moving on his face, and then stopped. "And besides, I gave you what you wanted. About me." He paused. "Or most of it. I never did that with a journalist before, and it'll probably be the end of me. But I did." The smile appeared full now; he had a good smile. "What is it you Yanks say? You owe me one."

I went over to the window. The small pale man was back in place, in front of the shop full of marine paintings. The rain was frailer now. Another Saracen rumbled down the street, and the pale man watched it go by. I turned to Steel.

"All right," I said. "Give me the letter."

He handed it to me; the letter was thick. Bills, perhaps. A long message. Steel turned away from me, as if he had run out of words. He glanced at the top of the bureau, and lifted the volume by Stendhal.

"Stendhal," he said. "*On Love*." He smiled. "Christ, Americans are very strange."

"Stendhal was French," I said.

"They're strange, too."

"And so are the Irish."

"Strangest of all," he said, and went to the door.

He hesitated, then opened it. Two men were waiting outside. One was bald and heavy. The other was the big man who had slammed me against the wall in the rain, a few hours earlier. Steel nodded to them, and then turned to me. The green eyes were gleaming and curious.

"Tell me," he said. "Is it possible that Ron Guidry can ever have another year like Seventy-eight?"

"No way," I said.

"I didn't think so," he said, smiled for the last time, and went down the hall, with the bald man in front of him, and the big guy covering his back.

5 I napped for three hours and dreamed of masked men with metal-tipped wooden spears coming at me through the fog and the air loud with the sound of helicopters. The fog became jungle and I was splashing through a rice paddy with someone behind me, and then the ground gave way and I was sliding into a deep channel of mud, and my ex-wife was standing in the distance waving at me with a white glove. I called to her, but she just waved her limp glove, and I screamed as the mud enfolded me.

I woke up cold, drenched with sweat. I lit a Vantage and, sitting on the edge of the bed with the blankets over my shoulders, I rang room service for a bottle of John Powers and some tea. Then I went into the shower. The pressure was low, and the tepid water came in a heavy drip. I soaped and shaved under the water, drying myself with the small rough towel. Then I pulled a terrycloth robe over my shoulders and sat at the table to transcribe the tape. I worked until almost five in the morning, and then I went back to sleep. I didn't dream.

It was noon when I woke, but there was no change in the light. I washed and dressed and then went down to the lobby. In the dark crowded lounge, I saw the little man who had come out to the airport with Frank Houlihan. He was reading the *Irish Times* from Dublin, but he looked up when I came to the door. He hurried over.

"Where to?"

"Let's drive around."

"Frank's house?" he said. "Up the Whiterock Road?"

"A good place to start," I said. "But let's take a long slow ride going there. I want to make notes."

"Right," he said. "A long slow ride."

And so I went out into the city that had given birth to men like Steel and to human beings who could torture women and castrate children. We roamed around; I talked to people huddled in their homes in the New Lodge Road, the old women begging me not to use their names, the young, bold and defiant. There were shells of burnt-out houses in Ballymacarrat, and ruined stores in the Markets, and concrete stanchions and metal fences sealing off the Europa Hotel, where I'd stayed a few years before. I interviewed a middle-aged man whose chest was scarred with the letters UVF, a souvenir from the Ulster Volunteer Force. I called a newspaper man at the *Belfast Telegraph* and he gave me the latest numbers: more than two thousand dead since 1969, twenty thousand wounded, ninety-one thousand buildings destroyed, a billion dollars' worth of damage. "Have a nice St. Patrick's Day," the newspaper man said over the phone, "but for God's sake, Sam, don't use my name."

All of those things would go into my article, along with my interviews with the Protestants of the Shankill Road, their stories of IRA atrocities, their rage at the killing of Mountbatten, their belief in the eternal union with England, their fear of an unholy alliance of the Pope and the communists, and I would describe how wonderful this relationship with England had been for them: their unemployed standing on the corners of the Shankill, now that the Harlland and Woolf shipyards were slowly closing down, and the pathetic homes along Sandy Row, symbols of their exploitation, with toilets in the yard, and their children scrawny from malnutrition.

I also heard all the recycled myths fed to the public by the British propaganda services: the IRA guerrillas were funded by gullible Irish-Americans who didn't know the true story; Muammar Qaddaffi of Libya was training the Provisionals; the PLO had been sighted on the Falls Road, and there were Cubans prowling the hills of Armagh. The British knew these were lies; they also knew that most of the funding of the rebellion was done in Ireland itself, through bank robberies and the operation of IRA businesses in Catholic ghettoes. Nobody had to travel to the deserts of Libya to learn how to fight in Belfast or Derry; the young Irish of the North didn't need the PLO to tell them they should fight. But the propaganda was effective in England and America. That's all that mattered. Naturally, I also heard the biggest myth: that the IRA rebellion had managed to sustain itself because Irish-American politicians supported the cause of a united Ireland, and other American politicians were afraid of losing the "Irish vote." Most of these accusations were aimed at the Big Four: two Irish-American Senators, an Irish-American Governor and the Irish-American Speaker of the House. Every St. Patrick's Day for four years these men had issued a statement on the troubles in Northern Ireland. The statements were always moderate. They always condemned violence. But they supported a united Ireland, and so the British popular press had portrayed them as men who condoned the actions of the IRA. Down on the Shankill Road, that was a big part of the myth.

"It's those four big shots that's kept this goin'," a carpenter named Cartwright said to me. "All this rubbish about a united Ireland. . . ."

Driving and walking around the city, thinking about the Big Four and the nonexistent Irish vote, hearing the words of hatred, bitterness, despair, and sorrow, I wished that it would all be over soon. In this country, history was a curse, and so was religion, and I had come to stand with E. M. Forster: I did not believe in belief. Other human beings could believe that God was a tree, or the sun, or Mao Tse-tung, or a 1946 Servel refrigerator; I didn't care. But when their beliefs grew rancid with murder, I longed for a cold cleansing wind, a wind that here in Ireland would destroy all the churches and the collective Irish memory, a wind that would leave all of them, Catholics and Protestants, back in some innocent state, afraid in the night of storms and earthquakes and behemoths, but not of each other. If that wind had to tear the churches off the surface of the earth, then let the wind blow.

At dusk, I saw one final defiant piece of graffiti: "The Great Seem Great Because We Are On Our Knees." It was on a wall near Leeson Street, a Catholic neighborhood, but it could have been on any wall in any town in Northern Ireland, and in most of the hurting places in the world. And I knew that was part of the article, too.

In all the Catholic neighborhoods they talked about the new IRA offensive and the man they called Steel. He was the one they'd been waiting for. A hard man, they said, a cold man, a man only happy when killing Englishmen. I went into a bar on the Falls Road. The customers were singing "The Men Behind the Wire" and then shifted to a ballad about Steel:

The British Army brought their guns,
Helicopters, bombs in tons,
Throwing terror into every field.
But now the Brits are on the run,
The Provos now are having fun,
Commanded by the hard man known as Steel. . . .

The man I had met the day before would have hated that song, and not simply for its aesthetic failures. I thought about him and his dead wife and his mutilated son, and the hatred he carried around like luggage. And I knew that I was already sick of it, sick of Ireland, sick of the songs and the suffering. I would leave this bar and go to say goodbye to Frank and get the hell out. I thought about my daughter April living in a strange, neutral, mountain country far from home, a century from Ireland. I thought about the Mercedes I had rented for the drive to the far end of Lake Geneva. I tried to remember the route I would take into the mountains, and how good it would be to smell the pine trees of Switzerland in the early spring.

"Let me have another," I said to the barman. "One for the road."

"Where are y' off to?" he said, his phlegmy face trying to look interested.

"I'll end up in New York."

His face tightened. "Ach, it must be terrible there now. All them muggin's. I lived there ten years myself. Worked for the telephone company." He filled my shot glass, and tapped the wooden bar. "Had to leave. Couldn't take all them niggers."

He walked down the bar to fill some Guinness glasses.

27

I threw down the shot, and went out to the darkness of the Falls Road. The driver looked up from his *Irish Times*.

"Frank's house?" he said.

"Yeah. Frank's house."

I sat in the back, feeling sleepy. They were killing each other everywhere. Someone somewhere was calling someone else a nigger and that made it easy to kill him. And somewhere a nigger was getting ready to kill first. I wished I could find Steel and say goodbye to him and his war. His face filled my head, along with his last words, about a baseball pitcher who labored in sweet green ballparks on summer afternoons. I wondered what was in the envelope he had asked me to deliver.

And then, up the hill, on the part of the Whiterock Road that faces the cemetery, I could see the lights of the ambulance. They turned slowly.

"Oh, sweet Jesus," the driver said. "Oh, sweet Jesus."

We stopped about thirty yards short of the ambulance. I got out. A crowd of boys lolled on the sidewalk. Women were standing in the doorways of the row houses, the lights out behind them, to avoid making targets.

"Brendan!" a woman's voice screamed. "Our Brendan! Come here now! This minute!"

There were police at the door of number 87, and in the darkness I could see two British soldiers.

"You have business here?" one of the policemen said.

"Yes," I said. "My uncle lives here."

"Are you a Yank?"

"Yes."

"Uncle's name Frank Houlihan?"

"Yes."

"You're just a wee bit late," he said.

"How late?"

"He's dead."

6 The little man who drove us from the airport handled everything. His name was Willie Toner. He checked me out of the International and moved me to a small upstairs bedroom in Frank's house. He had the mortician pick up the body at the morgue, after Frank had been photographed and his death recorded. He set up the wake in the front parlor, and he spread the word around the city that Frank Houlihan had been murdered, his throat cut from one ear to another.

For three days, they came to say goodbye: old soldiers who had known Frank as a boy; women who had known him in other ways; the young men who had revered Frank as a model and a hero, and who must have known that on some bloody midnight, death would come to them, too. The wake was not joyous; the myth of the glad and noisy Irish wake was another one of those sly lies invented to make the Irish somehow less than human. The men smoked too much, and talked quietly among themselves; the women watched the men, afraid of what might be coming. There was some soft keening late on the second night, when one of the older women began to call up the old pagan sense of loss, and the sound you heard was of pipes played at marches—the evocation of a thousand years of hard history and too many funerals. But for the most part, the wake was sober and sad.

I worked in the tiny upstairs room, rewriting the article, folding in the story of Steel, and adding the story of Frank Houlihan. It was a personal piece now. In a way, I was exorcising some guilt, and trying to channel my rage. If I hadn't come to Ireland on this trip, and hadn't been seen with Frank Houlihan, perhaps he would have died in bed, hugging his old dream to himself like an extra blanket. Perhaps, feeble with time, he would have stepped off a curb into the path of a speeding bus. The Woodbines might have killed him, or the bone-damp weather. But as I wrote, the rage did not diminish; it grew. I understood better why so many of the young men of the Provisional IRA had acted so

29

often as if they were truly mad. They had good reason. They were mad. They had been driven into that high white region of the mind where the grays of reason no longer exist, and you want to hurt, maim, destroy, obliterate. When I was young, I'd felt those emotions in a lot of places; older, tempered by the complexity of the world, I'd learned to cage them. In the upstairs room in my uncle Frank's last house, I was having trouble making the welds of the cage hold. I wanted to hurt someone back. It was now my war, too.

On the third night, Steel appeared in the upstairs room. The mourners were gone. Willie Toner was downstairs in the kitchen, clearing away the tea cups and the crumbs of the soda bread, and emptying the ashtrays. Steel didn't knock.

"I wanted to say I was sorry," he said.

"I knew you were," I said. "You didn't have to come here. They must be watching the house."

"I came in the hearse," he said. "They're all downstairs now, with the coffin."

He smiled thinly. He was a little too pleased with himself, the way actors are after a good performance. I didn't like it. I asked him what he wanted.

"I just wanted to say I'm sorry," he said soberly. "Nothing more."

"Thank you."

"I suppose there isn't much more to say," Steel muttered.

"Yes, there is," I said.

"What's that?"

"Who did it?"

He stared at his hands.

"We know the Brits spotted him with you," he said quietly. "That's not news. You know that, too. And of course the Brits know his background. They've had him in and out of prisons for years. But the Brits wouldn't do this. It's too risky. If they got found out, they'd be wrecked by the press."

"So?"

"There's a Red Hand faction of the UVF," he said. "It looks like their work. Our people are working on it. If we can find out with precision who did it, we'll act."

"I hope the operative word is precision," I said. "No dead children. No horrified wives."

"We try."

"Why Frank? They know he hasn't been active."

Steel sighed. "It doesn't matter to them," he said. "They know your work. You can write ten million words about everything from Vietnam to the sex life of snails. If you write one article about Ireland, and they don't agree with it, you're beyond the pale. You've written a dozen over the years."

"So they killed Frank to get at me?"

"I think so."

"That doesn't make much sense."

"This is Ireland."

He was silent for a moment. Then: "I suppose there isn't much more to say. I could give you the usual, about how he died for Ireland. And in a way, I'd be telling the truth. But it's a song I've sung too often. The edge is gone."

I shoved the bottle of Bushmill's at him. "Have some whiskey."

"I told you I didn't drink."

"Suit yourself."

He stared at me for awhile, and then the emerald eyes drifted around the small room, taking in the narrow celibate bed of Frank's last years, the dressing table, the picture of Jesus on the wall, hands bleeding and hearts bare, an icon of pain.

"There's the bloody problem," he said, nodding at the picture. "He's the one behind it all. We were perfectly happy people until St. Patrick arrived on these shores and filled us full of death and redemption."

I couldn't argue with that theory of Irish history.

"I think I'll have some whiskey myself," I said. "It never does me any good, but it's better than staring at you."

"I'm not much to stare at."

"Who the hell is?" I said.

So we sat for awhile, and I drank some whiskey. It didn't make me feel any better. And then Steel got up. It was as if the two of us had finished some unpleasant duty.

"Well, I'm off," he said.

"Thanks for coming by."

He paused at the door. "And you'll deliver that letter?"

"Yes," I said. "I gave you my word."

With that, he was gone.

In the morning, a dozen young men in black berets arrived at the house. They were an honor guard for Frank, men whose faces were so well known to British intelligence that they could risk being seen in public. They loaded Frank into a hearse. The coffin was plain pine, as Frank had wished, and there was to be no funeral mass, as he had wished. The hearse moved slowly down the Whiterock Road, past the Protestant cemetery, heading for the Falls Road. The young Provos accompanied the hearse. As the only family member, I walked immediately behind the gleaming black car, and when I looked over my shoulder, there were suddenly people as far as I could see.

I recognized some faces from the wake, but there were many others, young and old. A fine rain began to fall. We turned right on Falls Road, and marched in silence to Milltown Cemetery. There I joined the Provos and lifted the coffin out of the hearse. We walked through the tombstones carrying the clumsy pine coffin. Up ahead on a small knoll, beside a freshly-dug grave, there were more men in black berets, and a Uihleann piper making sounds as sad and mournful as history. We reached the graveside, and a priest appeared. He had a pouched florid face and dirty brown paratrooper boots under his black robe. He began to pray quietly. All heads bowed. A few of the crowd had the quick greedy eyes of cops. The prayer ended. Three of the men stepped forward and produced revolvers. They fired three rounds each in farewell. Birds fluttered and cried in the trees. The pipes stopped. It was over now; they lowered Frank into the Irish earth.

All I had to do now was leave, to go to Switzerland and see my daughter, and then return to the safety of New York. That was all. Except for the part of me that wanted to get even. Someone, somewhere had to pay for the death of Frank Houlihan, and I would be happy to be the man who collected the debt.

7 In the Geneva morning I had breakfast in the room, thick coffee and light *croissants*. The sky was the color of slate, the lake a dark dirty green. The shutters were open. I could see the grim spire of St. Peter's Cathedral, where John Calvin had preached his way into a heartless theological dictatorship, and I could feel his bleak, chilly presence seeping through the bones of the old city. Poor Jesus: he had preached love in a desert country, and for centuries, cold men had turned that love to stone in all the cities in Europe; Ireland was the last place where men were still killing to enforce the grim message. I worked all morning on the article, trimming and expanding, until it felt finished, and I was glad to be rid of Ireland.

After lunch, I drove along the edge of the lake, heading east, passing all those permanent monuments to the century's failure: the old headquarters of the League of Nations, where I had once seen peacocks strutting on summer lawns; stained concrete buildings belonging to various impotent international organizations; the dense thicket of the Jardin Botanique; and the villas of the exiles, the most terrible failures of all. Their houses huddled against the mountainsides, filled with people escaping taxes, revolutions, failures, changes of government, and broken marriages. They had purchased asylum and neutrality in the country of money. When I checked into the Beau Rivage a bellboy told me that one visiting Arab sheikh had given him a five-hundred-franc tip. That was roughly three hundred dollars. The young man seemed smugly pleased with himself, as if, like Calvin, he truly believed that salvation did indeed come from individual effort and the Arab had only paid him what he deserved. I remembered, as I pushed along the edge of the lake, that Rousseau had written *The Social Contract* here, in this city of moral angularities and cuckoo clocks. Rousseau was a man who wanted human rules. Money was not a rule, but only a fact. And in Switzerland all facts were neutral.

After an hour, I passed the castle of Chillon, where Byron's prisoner remained entombed by words and rhyme. And up ahead, I could see the snow.

At Vevey the road climbed into the mountains. Traffic was slowed by tour buses and Fiats crowned with ski racks. The snow swirled now, driven by a mountain wind. I came to a crossroads, with a one-pump gas station. An attendant filled my tank, as I watched a horse-drawn hay wagon move slowly down the mountain, backing up traffic for a mile. The horse wore blinders and a look of weary determination. The drover was young, with thick gloves and a yellow scarf masking his face. He nudged the horse to the right, through a gate marked by two white stone posts, up a snowy walk. In the distance, through the snow, I could see the outlines of a farmhouse. Lights were glowing inside the house, like signals of refuge.

I paid the attendant for the gasoline and drove the last eight miles to the town where my daughter was leading her separate life.

I waited at the top of a long, sloping, flagstone path, trying to read the Paris *Herald*, while young women clumped by on the hard-packed snow of the main street of Villars-sur-Ollon. In their heavy boots and down jackets, they looked as clumsy as adolescents, the boots making a squeaking sound as they walked, their skis new and shiny, small steamy clouds issuing from their mouths as they chattered in French and German, Spanish and English. As they passed the *pâtisserie*, the street narrowed, and all the young women merged into a pointillist mass of green and orange and purple, the waxed skis bobbing above them like the pikes of some medieval army. It was as if Brueghel had arrived with his paint box to splash some color against the neutral gray of the Swiss landscape. He must have put some young men in his picture, too, but I don't remember seeing them.

I scanned the sports page. Basketball didn't interest me at this distance, and the baseball chatter was about money and contracts, instead of young kids trying to hit curve balls in the springtime. I read a movie review by Tom Quinn Curtiss and some turgid editorials reprinted from *The New York Times* and *The Washington Post*, and gradually worked my way forward into the news section. There were the usual deadening reports from Moscow, Washington, and Peking, and some boilerplate from the campaign trails in various American states.

Down at the bottom of the fifth news page was a little item from Belfast. Two guards from the Crumlin Road Jail had been shot to death in broad daylight on their day off from work. British Army authorities said the Provisional IRA had taken credit for the killings. This brought to eight the number of prison guards killed in Northern Ireland since the beginning of the year. Meanwhile, four Protestant teenagers, two of them only sixteen, had been sentenced to fifteen years each for murdering a Catholic hot dog vendor. As they were led from the courtroom they shouted, "Up the UVF!"

The AP story did not explain that the UVF stood for the Ulster Volunteer Force, a small but deadly Protestant paramilitary force. Nor did the story explain that the UVF was responsible for turning the struggle in Northern Ireland into a religious battle; when the IRA killed a British soldier, the UVF responded by killing a Catholic. Any Catholic. It didn't matter whether that Catholic was connected to the IRA or a staunch Tory. He was a Catholic; so they killed him. Only one outfit was more deadly than the UVF; the British Special Air Services, or SAS. Their specialty was counter-terror, which was a polite way to describe political murder. They located people who they believed were involved with the IRA and then they killed them, sometimes with bombs, sometimes with notes left behind blaming other IRA factions. Never in a court of law. All the techniques developed in Malaya, Aden, Cyprus, and Palestine were used by the SAS; they made the UVF look like a youth gang.

Obviously, nothing had changed in the twenty-four hours since I'd left Belfast. I folded the paper, and looked out at the landscape, and waited for my daughter.

To the right, tiny dots of color moved down the slopes of distant mountains into the valley that gradually fell to Lake Geneva. Skiers. On my left, the Alps climbed away to Italy and I imagined Frederic Henry rowing his boat across Lake Como, Caporetto behind him, Catherine Barkley beside him, having said his farewell to arms. They had declared a separate peace and chosen a place of beauty and refuge; but Hemingway had written a tragedy, of course, and in a tragedy, someone always dies. Usually a woman. From that height Lake Geneva resembled a small gray pond, but the mountains were very sharp and clear in the cold February air, with nothing tragic about them, and I pictured a half-million industrious Swiss chambermaids rising early each morning to scrub them clean for the visiting foreigners. The foreigners came for a variety of reasons; but in this season they came primarily to ski. And all around me the skiers bubbled with excitement. The only English phrase I heard was "good powder," but the language of skiing meant nothing to me. Skiing wasn't my sport. There were no mountains where I came from, and no money to go to the mountains either. Good powder was something you put in a bullet.

Then I heard a muffled school bell ringing from within the low gabled building at the foot of the flagstone path. There was a moment of suspended time, without sound or movement, and then the double doors of the Collège Beau Soleil slammed open, and the children of the boarding school broke into the courtyard, shouting wildly in English and French. The boys packed fat wet snowballs and threw them at girls, and some tumbled their friends into the snow-packed fountain while others drifted behind a clump of pine trees to smoke sly cigarettes. Then I saw April's golden skin, her mother's raven hair bouncing in the cold breeze above the English-cut coat, her lustrous dark eyes searching for me through the swirl of unleashed kids.

"April!"

She turned and saw me, and then ran up the stone path in a wordless rush, her face blank, her jaw hanging loose. She crashed into me, and I lifted her, whirling her around and kissing her on the cheeks.

"Daddy, oh, Daddy, oh, Daddy, oh, Dad."

"Hello, sweetheart."

"I thought you wouldn't come. I thought something would happen. I thought the plane wouldn't come or there'd be a snowstorm in Geneva or—"

"It's okay, sweetheart. Don't cry. It's okay."

She cried anyway, burying her head against my neck. She was almost twelve, but in that moment she was the three-year-old who once played in the living room of an apartment on Bank Street in the Village, during that brief difficult time when we all lived together. I patted her on the back, wishing that she could be with me all the time, back in New York in the loft in Soho, wishing that she had not ended up in boarding school in these chilly Calvinist uplands, wishing that her loneliness and mine could have some fresh new mutual resolution.

"Let's get some lunch," I whispered.

"Okay, Dad," she said, and glanced behind her to see whether the other children had watched her cry. I put an arm around her shoulder, cutting off her potential audience, and then slipped her a handkerchief. She dried her tears as we joined the parade of skiers, walking past the yogurt store, the *cinéma*, the *tabac*, down into the narrow medieval main street with its expensive overhanging apartments, and then out into the wide square around the railroad station where the trolley waited to carry skiers to the mountaintops.

"You really look good, sweetheart," I said. "You must be the tallest almost-twelve-year-old in Europe."

She smiled: "Well, it's sure not from the food, Dad."

"What? You don't like French food?"

"Uck."

I laughed and so did she, and then we were in front of a restaurant called the Sporting. A sign advertised pizza.

"So how about a pizza?"

"Oh, *yes*," she said brightly.

"Have you been in this place?" I said. There was a large aquarium out front of the courtyard, full of glum river trout destined for dinner plates. A kind of Death Row for fish.

"No, they don't let us go here without a parent."

"Well, what the hell. I'm a parent, so let's go."

The restaurant was half full, and we went past the kitchen into the large main room and sat by a window. It was all wood and glass and very Alpiney. We could see most of the town of Villars, and the road climbing from the floor of the valley and the plain beyond. The menu was in English and French, and I let April order. Her French was flawless, although the word for pizza was still pizza, and Orange Crush was Orange Crush. Whiskey with water on the side was a bit more complicated, but she placed the order with a sense of command that I envied. At her age, I couldn't order a dog to sit. The waitress was a short thick blonde with freckles and large feet, dressed in the sort of native costume you never see worn by a single native. She took the order and walked heavily away. There was an awkward silence. Then April looked straight at me.

"How come you're here, Dad?" she said.

"Because of your letter. You said you wanted to see me and talk to me." I lit a Vantage. "That, and because I didn't see you at Christmas."

Her face clouded, as if remembering her Christmas. Then: "I loved the books you sent me. You know something? My English teacher said *Crime and Punishment* was too advanced for me, but I read it anyway. All the way to the end. He was *shocked*."

She smiled in a pleased way.

"Well, that was a terrific letter you sent me about Raskolnikov," I said. "You really understood him."

"The *weird* thing was that I *liked* him," she said. "He

did such a terrible thing, but I *liked* him. I didn't want him to get caught or get hurt."

"That's because Dostoyevsky is a great writer," I said. "You like Raskolnikov because Dostoyevsky makes you like him."

"How does he *do* that?" she said, her face puzzled.

"Nobody really knows. The poor literary critics have written a million words trying to find out. Dostoyevsky's one of those writers who writes words badly and is greater than all the fancy dans."

She looked out at the distant mountains. "Raskolnikov reminds me of the students of Beau Soleil."

"Really?"

"Sure. All the kids would like to kill *someone*. At least once."

"Like who?"

"A teacher. A monitress." She paused. "Their parents. Each other. Just do it *once*. Just *try* it. Raskolnikov did what most of us are afraid to do."

"I hope you don't feel like killing anyone, sweetheart," I said, chuckling, and pulling a drag on the cigarette.

She smiled thinly. "Not anymore."

"Who did you want to kill?"

"You," she said flatly. "And Mom."

I laughed nervously. "I'm glad you changed your mind."

"Yeah," she said. "Me, too."

The waitress thumped up to the table and put the two small pizzas and the drinks down in front of us. I took a sip of the whiskey and then cut into the twelve-inch pie. Pizza is the most mysterious of all foods. You find it on sale all over the world now, but for me it never works anywhere except in New York. I don't care who makes it, as long as it's made in New York; some of the best pizza I ever had was made by a Puerto Rican in an Irish dance hall in Coney Island. Not even Italy gets it right, although the cooks at least try. But the Swiss didn't have a clue about making a pizza. The crust was too thin, and there was not enough cheese. The cheese wasn't mozzarella, so the long strandy texture was wrong, and the tomato sauce was watery, and the chef had covered the surface with chopped ham, olives, and mushrooms, as if an instinct for the baroque could disguise the flaws in the basic form. The thing didn't taste bad. It just wasn't pizza.

"Have you heard from Mom?" April whispered.

"No," I said. "Or at least I haven't talked to her."

"She moved to Spain," April added.

"I know," I said. "She sent me a Christmas card."

"I'm going there at Easter. To some town that starts with a T."

"Torremolinos," I said. "You should have a good time there. There's a great beach and some decent restaurants. It's terrible in summer, hot and sweaty and full of hot, sweaty, German tourists. But it's lovely in the spring."

"I wish *you* could come, too."

"Your mother's boyfriend wouldn't be too happy about that."

She made a face. "Please, Dad, not while I'm *eating*."

"He sounds like a nice enough fella," I said without much conviction.

"Come *on*, Dad. He's a *jerk*."

"Maybe you're right."

"He doesn't work. He just sits around getting a *tan*, and drinking. He doesn't *do* anything." She was working hard on the pizza. "He's . . . he's . . . *unemployed*."

She said the word as if it were a disease.

I sipped the whiskey.

"Sometimes that can be a hard job," I said.

"Now, *him* I'd like to kill," she said sullenly.

"Great idea," I said. "Maybe you could feed him one of these Swiss pizzas."

She giggled, and ate the pizza, and sipped her Orange Crush. Her table manners were European now, the fork in her left hand carrying the pizza to her mouth, avoiding all that clumsy hand-switching that Americans do, and her accent was flattening out into that mid-Atlantic sound that comes from nowhere. Some day I would have to teach her the language we spoke in Brooklyn as if it were a dead dialect; in a way, it was, with even the Brooklyn kids now learning to speak from television instead of from each other. She finished eating and stared out at the valley.

"I want to go home," she said, without looking at me.

"I wish that was possible, sweetheart."

"Why isn't it?"

The whiskey didn't help at all. "The way I live . . . it wouldn't be fair to you, April. In my job, I'm always moving around. I'm always going places. There'd be nobody there to take care of you."

"I can take care of myself."

"You probably can. But New York is a tough hard place. In a few years . . ."

"Everything will happen in a few years, won't it?" she said. "I can *drive* . . . in a few years. I can *work* . . . in a few years. I can go on *my own* . . . in a few years. All in a few years."

"You don't have to be in such a big hurry to grow up," I said. "It's not such a big deal to drive or work or be on your own."

She was silent for awhile, then: "I'm sorry, Dad. I must be making you feel terrible."

"You should say what's on your mind, and don't worry about me."

"I *do* worry about you. All the time. I worry about something *happening* to you. I worry about you getting *hurt*."

"I'm too old to get hurt anymore," I lied.

"You said in your letter you were going to Ireland."

I laughed. "I went last week, and here I am. Safe, and reasonably sound."

"But I thought they were *killing* each other over there," she said. "My social studies teacher said that—"

"Yeah, they kill each other from time to time. It's very complicated. But I just wouldn't let them kill me."

She seemed to accept that. I finished my whiskey and then asked the waitress to bring me a coffee and the check. She grunted. My eyes followed her as she marched away to the cash register in the front of the restaurant, and then my heart stuttered. At a corner table, across the wide, crowded room, was a fat man in a tweed coat. He was reading *Le Monde*, and poking a tiny spoon into a demitasse of espresso. He had a red moustache and ruddy cheeks. I'd seen him before: the fat man who had watched me go through customs when I landed in Belfast.

"What's wrong?" April said, following my look.

"Oh. Oh, nothing," I said, and switched to Bogart. "Let's blow this joint, shweetheart."

"You sound *just like him*."

"Listen, you fresh punk, don't make fun. Thish is the way I always talk."

The waitress was gone a long time. I turned my back to the fat man, wondering what the hell he was doing there. He must be Special Branch. Or Special Air Services. Or UVF. He must know about that goddamned letter that Steel handed me, the one I had in my jacket next to my passport, right over my heart. April and I talked some more about Dostoyevsky. She was enthralled to learn that the great man had written his greatest books after marrying his second wife, who was only nineteen years old.

"Oh, Dad!" she said, "there's still *hope* for you!"

I laughed at that, and then the check came and I paid cash to save time. I turned and faced the table at the far end of the restaurant. The fat man was gone.

For a couple of hours, as the sun vanished behind the mountains, April and I walked through the town and talked. We talked about the archaeology of Mexico, which she was studying, and the best way to ski deep powder, which I knew nothing about, and how Flaubert had helped teach Maupassant to write. We stopped in the book store, and I bought her two Simenons and *The Old Man and the Sea* in French. We played eight games of pinball in the lounge of one of the ski hotels, and she won six of them. And then, in the early dark, I walked back to school with her.

All the while, I was thinking about the fat man. He knew where she was now. Whoever he was. If he were Special Branch, he wouldn't dare make a move on her. But maybe he wasn't Special Branch. Maybe he was UVF.

Maybe he was some crazy splinter of the IRA, enemies of the Provos, rivals of Steel. I didn't give a goddamn what people tried to do to me; my daughter was another story. We got to the top of the flagstone walk, and I thought about just getting her to pack, and taking her with me. To New York. Or dropping her off in Spain to stay with her mother. But then I remembered the long, winding two-lane road down the mountain, turning on itself again and again, in loops and curves. There was no other way to get down to the lake. If the fat man wanted something that I had, if he wanted the envelope in my jacket pocket, he would probably try to take it from me on the way down the mountain. I didn't want April in that Mercedes if I had to drive for my life. I held her hand, and we walked down the steps to the front door. We could hear the muffled voices of children running in upstairs corridors.

"When will I see you again?" she said.

"As soon as possible, sweetheart."

She was trying not to cry. "Well, thanks for coming to see me."

"Maybe we can spend the summer together," I said.

"That would be nice," she said, withdrawing her hand from mine. "Have a good flight home."

She reached up and kissed me on the cheek, lifted the wrapped books in a sign of thanks, and ran into the school through the double doors without looking back.

I walked through the town to the parking lot beside the railroad station. The streets were empty now. I could hear the Bee Gees and Donna Summer singing from the jukeboxes of the hotels. My boots squeaked on the dry snow, and as I passed the book store, I wanted to turn around and get my daughter and take her to her own country.

But I didn't. I went to the parking lot and unlocked the silver-gray Mercedes. I got in, closed the door, and sat there for a long moment, jingling the keys in my hand. I considered opening Steel's letter, reading it, and then burning it. I could deliver the message with my mouth. But if that had been possible, Steel would have asked me to do it that way from Belfast. I sat there. If they had traced me to this mountain town, then they had followed me all the way from Belfast. That meant they knew my hotel in Geneva. They certainly knew this car. If they wanted to whack me out, they had had all day to work on the engine.

I looked at the other cars in the lot, and there were no steamy windows indicating witnesses. The bright rectangles of the railroad station beckoned like a center of civilization from the far side of the parking lot. My hands were sweating; I slipped the key into the ignition, and held my breath. But I couldn't bring myself to turn it. I got out of the car and walked to the station. Three young women were waiting with their skis for the last train. I didn't see a fat man. I used the men's room.

Then I hurried back to the car, got in, slammed the door, and turned the key. The car started. The engine purred.

I breathed out hard, and started down the mountain.

8 There were no lights along the narrow two-lane road leading to a hamlet called Chesières, and the forest was black under the moonless sky, blotting out the fresh snow. But after I drove through the town, I saw the first van. It was ahead of me, the taillights glowing like a pair of red eyes. I started to pass, and the van moved suddenly to its left, blocking the lane. I slowed, and then saw the white lights of the second van in the rear-view mirror, about ten yards behind me. Both vans were black, shiny, and new. It was very simple: they had formed a parenthesis, with me in the brackets. At some point in the darkness, they would close the parenthesis.

There were no other lights in the dull night shimmer of snow and the dark lines of the forest. The only lights were ours—mine and theirs.

Lights.

My headlights and taillights. And theirs.

Cutting my lights, I shoved the Mercedes into second, veering left, jamming the accelerator to the floor. There was just enough room for me to pass the first van, but if a truck, a cart, or a tin can were in that lane, I would be dead.

It was empty. I flew past the first van, roaring now, hurtling down that narrow road leaving the two of them behind me. I could see the glare of their lights in my mirror, appearing, disappearing as the road twisted on itself, and I kept searching for a cutoff onto a side road, or the place where I had stopped for gas that afternoon and watched a frozen boy drive a hay wagon.

Suddenly the gas station was on me. To the right were the two stone posts of the small estate I had seen in the afternoon, and I jerked the wheel, narrowly missing the post to the left of the entrance, and went fifty feet at top speed into the darkness. A huge hulking shape was ahead of me, and I swerved to avoid it, braked, spun, heard the squeal of my own tires, and then stopped. Beside me was that hulking shape—a barn.

I rolled out of the car, staying low, wishing I had a gun. I raced to some shrubbery, dove flat into the snow and saw the two vans coming hard down the road. They had their brights on, but I could see no faces. They rushed past the gas station, and vanished into the black night.

I hurried back to the Mercedes. I had to get my daughter.

The headmaster was an American who had been away from home a long time. He was in his fifties, and when I told him I wanted to take April out of school for a week or so, he was surprised. When I told him it was because someone might try to kidnap her or hurt her, he was astonished. Such talk was the currency of movies, not of the placid steady world of mountain schools.

"I'd like her to pack quickly," I said.

"Whatever you say," he murmured, and disappeared down the wood-paneled corridor, looking domestic and old in a bright green bathrobe. Wood was everywhere, all highly polished, with mirrors and framed photographs of graduating classes. The building seemed thick with the unseen presence of sleeping children. I picked up a three-month-old copy of *Paris Match* and leafed through it, my eyes shifting from the slick pages to the door. In a rational world, I would simply call the police and tell them that somebody was trying to kill me. Or harm me. Or do some other goddamned thing to me. But it was not a rational world; I had learned that long ago. If I went to the Swiss police, I'd have to tell them what had happened. But I couldn't explain about the IRA, and the letter in my pocket, and the fat man in the Sporting. And if someone was after me, and that someone was a member of the UVF, or the British Special Air Services "counter-terror" outfit, that someone could make life dangerous for me. I had something that someone else wanted. It was as simple as that. I didn't like police stations anywhere in the world, particularly when I was being asked questions. The best thing was to go. Go in speed and silence. Go. And take my daughter with me.

I looked up. April was standing in the doorway in a blue down jacket, her eyes widening out of sleep as she saw me. The headmaster was carrying her bag. His mood had not improved.

"Daddy, where are we going?"

"Away for a few days, sweetheart," I said, and hugged her. Then I turned to the headmaster. "Is there another road down this mountain? I don't want to go through Chesières."

"Yes," he said, "but it's complicated. And with this snow, I don't know. . . ."

He gave me the directions in great detail, describing green farmhouses and yellow chalets and large trees, none of which would do me much good in the dark. I tried to remember everything, and then I thanked him, and said I would let him know soon about April's return. April and I walked out through the snow to the car, which I'd parked behind the school building.

It took us almost two hours to get off the mountain

through the network of back roads. The snow was whirling and violent, as if challenging the mountain, trying to bury it and all its arrogant inhabitants. I moved slowly, searching for those landmarks and turnoffs, and finding most of them. We saw no traffic, and there were no lights in the towns. When we came out into the valley floor, April was asleep again, her head on my lap.

I drove fast along the wide main highway, leaving behind the flat snow-covered farms, and curving along the lake, with the mountains always to my right, their peaks lost in the storm. A few cars drove by in the eastbound lane, skis lashed to their rooftops, but most of the world was asleep. After awhile, I could see the dull distant glow of Geneva.

9 The night clerk handed me the heavy brass key and told me there were no messages. He seemed surprised when I asked him to prepare the bill. The Swiss want their lives and their businesses to run like watches, without deviations; and I was deviating about twelve hours too early. He told me he would have to charge me for the full day, and when I said I knew that, he said that he just wanted me to know. I glanced around the empty lobby and asked if there was a bellman available. Yes. Send him up in twenty minutes, I said. He nodded stiffly, and April and I went to the elevator. When we got out on the sixth floor I took off my coat and laid it between the doors, to hold the elevator. If there were other guests waiting in the lobby for this car, to hell with them.

"Wait here," I told April. "Right in front of this elevator. If you hear anything—noises, shouts, a fight, any goddamned thing—get on the elevator, go to the lobby and tell El Creepo down there to call the cops."

"Right," she said, calm and delighted, rooting for trouble.

"And listen," I said, "don't *you* start anything, hear?"

She smiled and I walked down the carpeted corridor to

room 614. I listened at the door, and heard nothing. Trying not to breathe, I slipped the key into the lock. I turned it until there was a dull metallic click. And then I shoved it open, dived inside, rolled on my shoulder, turned over and came up in the space between the beds.

It was quite an entrance, but the room was empty. Recently empty. They had already been there. From my vantage point on the floor, I could see clothes strewn around, bureau drawers hanging open at a downward angle. I got up, and saw the scattered bits of my article, like yellow confetti, on the rug. Cocksuckers. The tape recorder was still there, but the cassette of my interview with Steel was gone. I stepped into the bathroom. Someone with a paint can had sprayed UVF on the mirror over the sink.

I went into the hall and called April. She came on a run, holding my coat, clearly disappointed. She wanted to rumble.

"Sorry I left this dump in such a mess," I said. "Help me pack, okay?"

"Sure."

She packed, and I called the airlines. There was a Swissair flight to Barcelona at seven A.M. and they said they could book me through to New York on a TWA flight an hour later. I reserved two seats to Barcelona and one to New York. Then I placed a call to Torremolinos. A man answered.

"Mrs. Briscoe, please," I said.

"*Quién es?*" he said grumpily.

"*Señor* Briscoe," I said. I always loved that part when I called her. He grunted and went away, and then she came on the line.

"Sam?"

"Hello, Elaine."

"Sam, it's four o'clock in the morning."

"I know. Listen, I'm calling from Geneva." I shifted to Spanish in case there was anybody listening from the lobby switchboard. "I'm arriving with April at the Barcelona Airport at nine thirty-five," I said in Spanish. "Swissair

Flight 16. I can't explain why, but I want her to stay with you for awhile, *entiende*?"

Her voice became annoyed and sharp. "Sam! She's in school. She could lose a whole term if you take her out now."

"She could lose her life if she stays."

"You mean you've gotten her involved in one of your goddamned melodramas, Sam?"

"I'll explain when I see you. Will you meet us?"

She sighed, and went back to English. "Goddamn it, Sam."

I gave her the flight number and the arrival time again in Spanish and said goodbye. April had packed everything. Then there was a sharp knock at the door. I motioned April into the bathroom, and again wished I had brought my gun.

I jerked the door open. The bellman stood there, his sallow Italian face lengthening in surprise.

"Hello, there," I said. "We're checking out."

When we came through customs at Barcelona, Elaine was in the waiting room, like a snapshot from the past. She had waited for me in a lot of airports in those first years, when we were just married and I was a kid reporter flying home from wars and riots. In the beginning, I suppose, it had been exciting for her, not knowing what would ever happen, indulging in the melancholy ritual of separation and reconciliation. But after a few years, it must have become a bore. I came home once from Saigon, after a month away, and she wasn't at the airport. When I came home from the Munich Olympics, she wasn't at the airport and she wasn't at the apartment on Seventy-third Street either. She was never there again.

"Mother!" April shouted, and broke through the crowd and ran to Elaine. The two of them ignored me, embracing and talking vividly among the excited crowd of homecoming Spaniards. I went to get April's suitcase from the baggage area. When I came back, Elaine finally turned to me.

"Hello, Sam," she said coolly. "You've got a half hour, right?"

"Right."

She shook my hand in an awkward way. I inspected the familiar raven hair, the burnished copper highlights, the green eyes. Those goddamned green eyes. The three of us walked through the crowd to the bar. She waved, and a small Andalusian chauffeur came over and wordlessly took April's bag. Jesus Christ, I thought, she's more beautiful than ever. Her skin was deeply tanned and moist from creams, her body lean and trim from tennis. I thought about parts of that body which I'd once known better than my own, and then pushed the images out of my head.

"Well," she said, as we sat down at a table in the cool dark bar.

"Well, what?" I said.

"What's this all about?"

She arched her right eyebrow, the way she always did when she didn't approve of the things I did with my life. She used to arch her eyebrow at me a lot.

"I'm not sure what it's all about," I said. "But I've been working on a story about the IRA. A man I saw in Belfast followed me to Villars. So he must know what school April is in. And though nothing might happen, I don't want to take the chance. I don't know who the man is, but I don't think he's a guardian angel."

I didn't mention the two vans chasing me down the mountain, or the violated look of my room in Geneva.

"You sure you're not catching galloping paranoia in your old age?" she said.

"It could be," I said. "But I do have enemies."

"Maybe you need help. I know a good doctor in New York."

"Someone did make a mess of his room in Geneva, Mother," April said.

A waiter came over. Elaine glanced at April, then at me. "Can I buy you a drink?" she said.

"No," I said, "this round is on me."

I ordered a Coke for April, a whiskey for me, and a

vodka tonic for Elaine. April excused herelf and went to the ladies' room. I shifted my chair to watch her. She was going to be tall.

"You look terrific, Elaine," I said, without looking at her.

"You're looking well yourself, Sam."

"You like Torremolinos?"

"Not very much. But it's not all glitz and glitter, you know. It's not Miami or Acapulco or Cannes. And by the time it does go that way, I'll be gone."

The waiter brought the drinks and I paid him in dollars. He looked unhappy, but took the money anyway.

"And this new guy?" I said.

"He's harmless," she said carefully, "and that's all right with me."

I sipped the Scotch and watched the door to the ladies' room. A fat lady came out. Two American girls went in.

"I'm sorry you don't write the column anymore, Sam."

"I got too old."

She laughed. "We're all getting older, even April." She was looking across the restaurant at April, who had come out of the ladies' room and was moving confidently through the tables of waiting passengers.

"Show me someone who's getting younger," I said, "and I'll give you a million bucks. Of course, I don't have the million and you don't need it. But—"

"I'm glad to see you *smiling*, at least, Dad," April said. "You looked so *gloomy* before."

"It must be the company," I said, and hugged her. Elaine made a face as she sipped the vodka and tonic.

"It's about time for you to board, isn't it, Sam?"

"Yeah."

She got up and took April's hand. "I guess we'd better get going," Elaine said. "I'll call you in New York."

We walked together to the door of the bar.

"April?" I said. "Excuse me for a minute, will you?"

"Sure, Dad."

She dropped behind us. The little Andalusian chauffeur returned. The bulge on his hip was reassuring.

"Listen, Elaine, I'm sorry about this. It screws things up, I know that. But I didn't plan it this way."

"You never planned anything in your life," she said. "So what's new?"

"This could be bullshit," I said. "I could be imagining this whole thing. But I did my best to be sure we weren't followed down here. Who the hell knows? If anything weird happens, call the cops. And keep the chauffeur around, the one packing heat."

"You still don't miss much, do you?"

"I'm a reporter. I'm fairly good about things I can see. It's the other things that get me in trouble."

I wanted to touch her hair, and bite the little pad of fat under her chin. Instead, I brushed her cheek with a kiss, as friendly as a brother.

"Who are these people anyway? The ones who are after you?"

"I don't really know," I said. "But I expect I'll be finding out real soon."

She squeezed my hand. "Well, watch your ass, okay?"

"I'd rather watch yours."

She smiled, and I leaned over and kissed April goodbye. I went into the departure lounge, and looked back once, but they were gone.

10 All the way across the Atlantic, I worked at reconstructing the destroyed article about Ireland. I'm not one of those magnificently blessed gentlemen reporters who can spend a few weeks chatting with men on Death Row, say, and then, without notes, quote from them in enough precise detail to fill a book of five hundred pages. I don't have total recall, certainly not about the words and lives of others. I need notes, scrawled in spiral pads, recorded on tape, jotted on index cards that hide in the inside pockets of jackets. But all such notes were gone for this one, and the deadline was the next afternoon. So I ordered a whiskey from the stewardess, and wrote at speed in a schoolboy's composition book that I'd bought at the Barcelona airport. Slowly at first, and then in a rush, the details of Ireland came back to me. I could hear the hard northern voices, connected intimately to the names of streets and bars and ruined places; I recounted what had happened to Frank Houlihan; and, filtered through memory, the presence and importance of Steel became clearer than ever.

His soft voice moved in my head, and I remembered his eyes and hands, the carefully anonymous character of his clothing, the almost aristocratic length of his nose, making him look as if he had stepped out of some eighteenth-century portrait to be badly fitted in modern clothes. He had been to America, had lived there for a long time; he knew enough about Ron Guidry to ask one sensible question about him. But more important, he possessed an iron will; through an act of that will he was making the IRA function in a way that it had not functioned in years, with efficiency and purpose. I had long since ceased to believe that history was some abstract inevitable stream; history was made by men and women, and in his way, Steel was one of those men, making history in one of the smaller outposts of the world.

I said all that in the piece, and an hour from Kennedy I was finished. I ordered another whiskey, and realized that I was the only passenger still awake. Carrying the composition book with me, patting my jacket to be certain I had Steel's letter, I went through the sleeping plane to the lavatory and washed my face. I felt suddenly very tired and drained. I had been gone only seven days but it felt like a year. In the morning in New York I would call an old friend who ran a typing service and would have the handwritten article typed on white bond paper, and while she was doing that, I would sleep. But not now. I went back to my seat and read Stendhal until we were on the ground. Stendhal knew almost everything. But he didn't know about Ireland or about the long tanned legs of ex-wives.

I leaned back in the cab, and as we pulled out of the airport onto the Van Wyck Expressway, I fell into sleep. In a dream, a large lumpy man was climbing through the window of the flat where we lived when I was a boy. He was dressed in black and carried a filthy canvas bag; his eyes were the color of lard. In a corner, my father was sitting in his maroon-and-gold easy chair, wearing a policeman's hat and reading a newspaper. But when I shouted to him for help, he did not hear me. The lumpy man with the lard-colored eyes looked at me and smiled.

I awoke with a start in the Midtown Tunnel. The cab slowed; only one lane was open, and I could see a large yellow Port Authority truck up ahead, its warning lights blinking urgently, while its rotary brushes cleaned the dirty tiles of the tunnel in the closed lane.

"You must be wiped out," the cabbie said. He was in his fifties, lean, and Jewish. He had a kind, exhausted voice.

"Jet lag," I said.

"Where'd you come from?"

"Europe. Ireland."

"I hear it's beautiful, that Ireland."

"Some of it. The North isn't so beautiful."

"Yeah," the cabbie said. "That's a mess. Imagine Catholics and Protestants killin' each other in this day and age? It sure is weird."

"Well, it's more complicated than that. It's not just Catholics against Protestants. But, yeah, it's weird."

As we came up out of the tunnel, I remembered to look more closely at the other cars in the clotted traffic. None of them was carrying a fat man with a red moustache. I was certain he was in one of the black vans that night in the snow, and that he'd wanted to kill me. But I wasn't certain why. It had to do with the IRA and the letter from Steel, but I didn't even know whether the men in the vans were British or Irish. I was certain of one thing: if they could find me, they would try again. And I was never a hard man to find.

The cab stopped at a red light at Fourteenth Street, and a Puerto Rican girl walked across the street. She was about eighteen, with long legs encased in jeans, tapering to a pair of cheap spiked heels. She was wearing a shiny black baseball jacket, and her golden face glowed with an almost heartbreaking beauty. She headed for the ruined streets of the Lower East Side, and I remembered again how dangerous it was in some New York neighborhoods for a girl to be beautiful. I knew—I had seen the corpses. In some vagrant way, I wanted to get out of the cab and rescue the girl. Galahad with a press card. But the light changed, and the driver gunned the engine into the savage traffic. Like everybody else, she would have to save herself.

The driver pushed on, struggling valiantly against the tide of banana trucks, double-parked cars, and ragged platoons of schoolkids crossing against the lights. By the time he dropped me at the loft on Spring Street in Soho, the meter said I owed him seventeen dollars. I gave him twenty-two dollars and carried my bag and typewriter to the freight elevator. Chamaco, the elevator operator, smiled a welcome.

"Hey, Mister Briscoe, you're back, man!"

He slapped me five. "Yeah, Chamaco. Home again. *Ćomo está?*"

"*Bien, bien. Y tú?*"

"Not so fuckin' *bien*," I said, as I closed the door and started up. "Anybody been around looking for me?"

"Nah. Jus' the mailman."

"Nobody weird hanging around the block?"

"Nah. Jus the reggala weirdos."

In the loft, I dropped the bag and typewriter near the door, beside Red Emma which was parked in my living room. I flicked on some lights. Red Emma is my car, a Jaguar XJ-5 that was one of the products of the only adult crap game I'd ever entered from which I'd come out a winner. That was the year Saigon finally fell, and I had sixty-five hundred dollars in expense money which General

Giap prevented me from spending on the girls of Tu Do Street. On the way home I stopped in Vegas, where I promptly hit twenty-eight straight passes, cashed my chips in, and left with a hundred and eight thousand dollars. With the money I'd bought the loft, furnished it, and added Red Emma to brighten up the evenings. I could have left her at Kennedy on the way to Ireland, but Red Emma is not the kind of lady you leave lying around. People like to borrow her. It's also not a good idea to leave any car around the Kennedy Airport parking lot for too long; racket guys have made the place their favorite cemetery, and you could come home to find some strange people in your trunk.

I put John Klemmer's new album on the phonograph, and laid my passport and Steel's letter on a shelf of the bookcase. I put the composition book on the bar, and, pouring myself a whiskey and soda, I took off my clothes and carried them into the bathroom, jamming everything into the hamper. Then I stepped into the shower and boiled myself clean. Today must be the fifteenth of March, I thought. That meant the piece was due tomorrow. In the shower, I told myself that first I would call the typist, and leave the manuscript with Chamaco to be picked up by a messenger, and then I would go to sleep. I was going to need the sleep before traveling over to Woodside to play mailman.

11 Queens is the great unmapped country of New York. All the other boroughs of the great city have been at least partially explored for a century, but only Jimmy Breslin has poled a boat down the rivers of Queens. Sharing the face of fish-shaped Long Island with Brooklyn, Queens is a confusion of numbered streets, avenues that go nowhere, and people who have moved so many times in search of safety that they are no longer capable of the dream of flight. It is a perfect haven for exiles. Exiles are, of course, different from refugees; refugees flee in anger, or

fear, just ahead or the winning side of the Czar's police, and after awhile, the anger ebbs, their children are born, they become immigrants, and the old country is forever behind them. But exiles never sink spikes into the new earth. They live in a suppurating wound that can only be closed by return. The old country is a daily reality and America only a parenthesis.

So Queens contains a hundred thousand Dominicans who dream of buying land beside the ocean sea; seventy-five thousand Colombians full of the high hazy smoke of mountain farms in the morning; thirty thousand Haitians sorrowing for the sound of bare feet slapping on country paths, while the old Gods tumble with each other in the forest. Queens also has the Irish. A lot of them. And Irish bars. A lot of them.

McDaid's was in Woodside under the El. I got there after midnight and parked Red Emma around the corner, a half-block from an all-night newsstand. The night was cold, the false spring gone with the afternoon sun. I picked up a *Daily News* and walked into McDaid's. They'd sent a copyboy to the typist's for my piece, and I'd only had to trim three paragraphs before leaving for Queens. The piece would run the next day, on the eve of St. Patrick's Day.

McDaid's was like a pub in Derry, on some imagined future evening when the final victory had been won and the Brits had departed forever. Through the noise and cigarette smoke, I could see a bar to the left, with men in tweed jackets and gabardine suits pressed three deep against its mahogany length. They were drinking pints of clear ale or draft Guinness. A few young women were squashed between them on stools. Two bartenders worked quickly, pulling pints, while a Schlitz sign bubbled over the cash register and reflected off the chased mirrors. There were a few lonely ones, too, staring at their reflections in the mirror or playing with change on the wet bar, night drifters in from the cold. Against the wall on the right, booths were packed with celebrating couples. In one of them, seven girls shared a pitcher of beer, waiting for men to make an approach, their freckled Irish faces glowing in the muted light. There were

St. Patrick's Day posters on all the walls, offering dances, protests, cabarets, and I counted seven Irish tricolors and three portraits of Patrick Pearse. On the jukebox a group called the Barleycorn were singing a song I'd heard a hundred times across the ocean. About half the crowd joined in the thunderous chorus:

> *Armored cars, and tanks and guns*
> *Came to take away our sons*
> *But every man must stand behind*
> *The men behind the wire.*

I was mumbling the words myself, when a tall redhaired waitress came over.

"Bar or table?"

"Uh, table, I guess."

Her ice blue eyes stared over a long aquiline nose and high cheekbones. She had brushed color onto her pale skin to accent the cheekbones. Her breasts were large for a thin girl, moving under a tight green blouse set off by the white straps of her apron.

"How many are you?" she said, in an even American girls's school accent.

"I'm alone."

"Then you can't have a table. Sorry."

"I have to see Jack McDaid."

She looked at me in a steady way. "He's not here."

"Is he expected?"

"Who are you?"

"My name's Briscoe. He might be expecting me."

She looked at me with a flicker of recognition now. For ten years my face had been pasted at the top of a newspaper column. I didn't write the column anymore, but sometimes they remembered my face.

"Well, he's not here. You can get a drink at the bar."

She walked over to the booth with the seven girls in it and lifted their empty pitcher. She had good solid legs encased in black stockings that didn't go with the waitress rig. She pushed her way through the outer ring of young men and made an end run to the bar. I drifted to that end, standing beside the service opening, and ordered a draft beer. The thin, moustached bartender wore a Pioneer pin on his shirt, a sign that he had taken the pledge never to drink. Such Irishmen are prized bartenders on the Irish saloon circuit, but I never trusted them to fix me a drink more complicated than a beer.

"What do you want to see him for?" the redhaired waitress said, as she waited for her pitcher to be filled. She didn't look at me, and barely moved her lips when she talked.

"I have a message for him."

"From who?"

"A man from the old country."

Her pitcher arrived, she lifted it, turned, looked at me toughly, and went by me to the booth. An instrumental jig and reel was playing now, with the Chieftains in full Celtic ride, and a lot of the customers were dancing. Four of the girls from the booth danced with each other, doing the ancient Irish steps as if they had learned them in an Irish studies course at Manhattan College. The waitress came back.

"Why don't you give the message to me?" she said, still not looking me in the eye.

"I don't even know your name."

"Sheila."

"Nice to meet you, Sheila. But I was told to give the message to Jackie McDaid. And you're not Jackie McDaid."

"And you might not be Sam Briscoe, either. You could be a cop. You could be from immigration. You could be just another goddamned degenerate."

"Or all of the above."

She fought off a smile. "Exactly."

I picked some nonexistent lint off my jacket. "On the other hand, I could have something very important to deliver."

"I doubt it," she said, lifting a tray full of whiskeys and soda bottles.

"I could be carrying something that would put some steel into a few backbones."

She didn't say anything. But her eyes held on me for a long beat, and then she lifted the tray and walked away. I watched her reflection in the mirror. She dropped off the tray, made some change, and then walked along the row of crowded booths, passing the jukebox, disappearing down some steps into a back room. I ordered another beer, and looked at the *Daily News*. Barleycorn was back on the jukebox and the crowd was singing again.

> *Armored cars, and tanks and guns*
> *Came to take away our sons*
> *But every man must stand behind*
> *The men behind the wire.*

I began to read an editorial about the fiscal crisis, and how disgusting it was to pay mere garbagemen a living wage, when I was tapped on the shoulder.

"You've got something for me?"

Jackie McDaid was taller than I was, redfaced and wide, with a vertical bar of eyebrow and a heavy northern accent. His thick fingers seemed uncomfortably attached to his hands. The sleeves of his white shirt were rolled up, and the veins of his arms stood out like cords.

"If you're Jackie McDaid, I do," I said. Sheila hovered in the smoky haze against the wall beside the juke.

"I'm Jack McDaid," he said.

"How do I know that?" I said.

He reached over and tapped a customer on the elbow with one of the big fingers.

"Hello, Jerry," he said. "How are ye?"

"Jack McDaid," the customer said. "Jase, I didn't see ye, mon, when I walked in."

"I wasn't here."

"You're lookin' wonderful, Jack. Jase, I haven't seen ye since Mountbatten got blitzed."

"You're lookin' fit yourself, Jerry," McDaid said. "And the missus?"

"Grand, she's grand. Jase, did you see the headline in

the Provo paper when they got Mountbatten? A picture of the bloody Queen and the headline says, '*One Fewer for Dinner!*' Jase, they're a hard lot, the lads."

"Aye," McDaid said, without moving his face. He turned to me. His eyes were brown but they weren't soft.

"I'm Sam Briscoe," I said. "I have an envelope for you, but I don't want to give it to you here." I smiled and then laughed a dumb dry laugh, in case anyone was looking. "I might have been followed. I'm just not certain."

He laughed out loud, as if I'd told him a truly fantastic joke, and draped an arm over my shoulder, while his eyes scanned the smoky saloon. Then he shouted at one of the bartenders.

"Harry, give us the delivery books from Seagram's, will ye, lad?"

The man nodded, reached into a cabinet beneath the cash register and removed a ledger. He handed it across the service area to McDaid.

"Come on," McDaid said loudly to me. "We'll settle this bloody thing now."

I followed him down the three steps through a narrow passage, past the lavatories and into the back room. There were more tables and chairs and a bandstand, but the room was empty and smelled of sour beer.

"If the bar business goes bad," I said, "you should try acting."

He shrugged while he opened an office door with a key. There was a desk inside, a phone, a chair, but nothing at all on the walls. He closed the door behind me, dropped the phony ledger on the desk, turned and faced me. I handed him the letter from Steel.

"Thanks," he said, holding the sealed letter.

"You're welcome," I said, feeling stiff in the company of this large humorless man.

"If you'd like a drink," he said, "just tell Sheila."

"I don't accept tips," I said.

He gave me a look. "Sorry, mate. I didn't mean it that way."

"Fuck it," I said.

"I appreciate what you've done," he said.

"Let me warn you," I said. "A fat man with a red moustache followed me to Switzerland, I think to get this envelope. He tried to take it from me. He might have come here, too. So watch it."

"That would be Redmond. Stanley Redmond. SAS. Special Air Services. A bloody murderer."

I told him what happened in Switzerland.

"We'll send someone to the town where your daughter goes to school," he said. "She'll be safe. Believe me."

I told him she was in Spain for the moment, and he wrote down the address in Torremolinos, along with the name of the school in Switzerland. Then he shook my hand.

"What's that waitress's name again?"

"Sheila. Sheila Rafferty. A good woman, for a Yank. If you'll pardon the expression."

I needed a drink. When I went back to the bar and ordered a beer, Sheila came over. The crowd was thinning out now. The singing was more out of tune.

"You can have a table now," she said. "If you want."

"Only if you join me."

"Fuck off," she said, and laughed.

"Such language from a nice Catholic girl."

"I'm not a Catholic anymore."

"Ah, a retired Catholic. The best kind."

"I was brought up a Catholic," she said, a smile moving tentatively across her face. "But I haven't believed any of it since I was fourteen."

"But you do have to admit the music was pretty damned good, and the popes always hired the best painters, right?"

"Do you want a table?"

"I'd rather have your phone number."

"It's in the book," she said, and walked over to an

abandoned booth to pick up empties and mop up spilled beer. I put the beer glass down on the bar and walked out to the street. The air was brisk and cold after the dense smokiness of the saloon. An elevated train screeched to a halt overhead, metal grinding against metal. I looked back and saw the blur of Sheila's face through the window. I gave her a little wave, and walked to the corner.

12 Red Emma was parked with her nose aimed away from the corner newsstand. As I pulled out, heading into the dark at the top of the street, I planned to make a pair of lefts to come around again at the El, and follow it to the bridge for Manhattan. Then parking lights suddenly lit up on a black car parked a half-block behind me. I drove slowly for a hundred feet, and then abruptly accelerated at the corner.

The car behind me accelerated, too. It looked like a Buick Regal. I made another left turn, and another, but those lights stayed thirty feet behind me. I came out at the El, doubled back past McDaid's to the newsstand, and was finally aimed at Manhattan. Two cabs were double-parked at the newsstand, waiting for fares.

Before I got to the corner, the light turned red, and I stopped. I reached under the seat for a tire iron and got out.

The Buick was stopped ten feet behind me. I sprinted to the driver's side. A blond man with a hard gullied face was alone behind the wheel, dressed in a blue checkered sports jacket. The window was rolled up tightly. I didn't wait for him to roll it down. I smashed the glass with the tire iron and reached in for his neck.

"Who the fuck *are* you, pal?" I said.

He was choking, and pulled away from my grip. "Hey, what you doin', man," he said in a southern accent. "You crazy?"

I lifted the button on his door, jerked it open, dropped the iron, and grabbed him with both hands. When I pulled him out of the car, he landed hard, face down on the asphalt. He started to get up and I hit him hard on the ear; he fell back, his legs splayed at an awkward angle. I glanced at the cabdrivers. Two of them were standing on the corner now, watching with their hands in their pockets.

"Get up," I said.

"I want the police."

"I'll give you a cop, you prick. I'll give you the whole fuckin' police department."

His hand moved inside his jacket, and I kicked him in the side of the head. He fell over and groaned, and I reached into the jacket. No gun. Just a sheet of paper in the inside pocket. It was folded four times. I ran my hands around his belt. This type always has a gun, and his was a .32-caliber Smith and Wesson automatic. I took it out of the hip holster and laid it on top of the car. He started to sit up, tamely. The traffic light turned green and then red again, but there was no other traffic. Smart people were all home in bed. I looked at the sheet of paper: a piece of stationery from the Plaza Hotel. The address of McDaid's bar was written on it in large rolling script. My name was underneath, and "red Jaguar." There were also directions from the Midtown Tunnel to Queens, and then to McDaid's. And the letters "CCL" were scribbled five times, the way people doodle when talking for a long time on a telephone.

"You came a long way for a glass of Guinness, didn't you, pal?"

"Ah don't have to say a goddamn theng t' yew."

"When the cops get here," I said, "you can explain the gun."

He grabbed the rear left fender of the car and slowly got up. The ravined face reminded me of a chief petty officer I served with in the Navy, years ago; I'd beaten him up, too, but I was eighteen then and it was a lot easier.

"What's a nice southern boy like you doin' out here in the New York boondocks, boy? Your type usually spends the nights at the whackoff parlors on Forty-second Street."

He turned his head, as if he were going to cry. And

then lunged for the letterhead, tore it from my hand and began to run. He could run. He took off in long-legged strides, and I was after him, as another train screeched around the bend of the El above us. He had a flat-out pumping runner's style, and he dodged the steel girders of the El like a soldier expecting a bullet in his back. Then he bounced up on the sidewalk across the wide street from McDaid's, running for the darkness. My heart was pounding, my legs hurting, my breath cigarette-thin, and I glanced at the now shuttered bar and saw Sheila starting across the street. She was dressed to go home. The two bartenders were getting into a car.

And then for one frozen moment everything was silent and I rose into some high bright place, floated there for a long time and then fell to the ground, deafened by the tearing, breaking whoosh of an explosion.

I went away again, to a place without sound. When I returned I could hear screaming, and running feet, and shouts of alarm, the squeal of a train, and car horns. I got up.

The front of McDaid's was gone. Smoke tumbled out of the blackness, and I could see orange flame deep within the bar. The smoke burned my throat. My eyes watered. The Southerner was gone. But the cabbies had come running over to the bar, and some of the other neighborhood joints had emptied; I could see one of McDaid's bartenders sitting against a parked car in his topcoat, his eyes dazed. And then I saw Sheila Rafferty. She was screaming at the smoke.

"Jack! Jack!"

But the flames were building now. Two muffled explosions sounded from deep inside, and a series of pops as bottles exploded, and then the roof fell in. We could hear sirens coming; a squad car jerked around the corner, its lights whirling. Two young cops jumped out.

"Jack McDaid's still in there!" Sheila screamed. "He's in there, he's in there!"

"Take it easy, lady," one of the cops said politely.

"But there's a man in there!"

"If there is, we can't get to him, lady. We gotta wait for the firemen."

The other cop was moving everybody back, when Sheila turned and saw me. Her face was the color of bone. She locked eyes with me for a second, turned away to look at the bar, then turned in the direction of the deeper sirens of the approaching fire engines. Walking at an odd angle, her body facing the bar, she came over to me.

"They did it," she said in a remote voice. "They've got Jack."

"Maybe not," I said. "Maybe he got out the back way."

"There is no back way," she said. "He had it sealed."

The firemen came off their trucks on the run; three of them plunged straight into the smoke, carrying hand extinguishers while others hooked up the big hoses from the pumper to a hydrant. One final smothered detonation rumbled from the back of the bar, and the three firemen hurried back outside. Alarmed, Sheila grabbed my arm. And then removed it in an embarrassed way.

"They did it," she said. "They came all the way from Belfast and they got him."

I took her elbow and moved her back under the El toward my car. The black Buick was gone and so was the automatic I'd left on its hood. Sheila looked back at the long high arc of water pouring now from the hose. The water sizzled and crackled on the hot burning mess, and ash floated into the stained night air. I picked up the tire iron.

"Come on," I said. "I'll drive you home."

"I don't want to go home."

"Then come home with me."

"All right," she said. "I'll go home with you."

13 Sex and death are intimately connected. Orgasm, someone once said, is the little death, the journey to the beyond. But when I took Sheila Rafferty home to the loft, I had no little death in mind. She was stunned into silence, and I gave her the couch, a pillow, some blankets, and went alone to the sleeping bay. I drifted slowly into sleep, replaying the night's violent events, and then suddenly, wordlessly, she was beside me. Her naked body was full, loamy, driven by need, desperate for life, consolation, pleasure. I didn't really matter, except as an instrument for satisfying her need. She fingered my hair, brushed her pink hard-nippled breasts against my face, held me against her belly, thrust against me with her wetness, saying nothing, panting, making deep animal sounds of loss and need. When she came at last, her body arched and bent away from me as if broken, and her high-pitched throbbing voice slowly lowered into deeper moans and then into injured wracking sobs. After awhile, she was quiet.

"I didn't mean to do that," she whispered. "I didn't come here to sleep with you."

"Don't explain."

"I don't know why. . . . Oh, God, I feel so dirty."

"Don't be ridiculous."

She began to cry again, and I held her close to me until she was cried out. She reached down then, and touched me.

"I was so involved with me," she said, "I forgot about you."

"It's okay."

"No, it's not," she said. "It's not fair."

She came to me more slowly now, the need transformed into something more remote. Now she was hands, mouth, belly, hair, kneading, caressing, enveloping; but Sheila Rafferty was no longer in that bed. When she was finished, and fairness had been served, she asked me for a cigarette. I handed her a Vantage, and lit it for her. She inhaled greedily, and lay back, pulling the sheet up to her chin.

"Why don't you tell me what really happened out there tonight?" I said.

"I don't want to talk about it."

"If you don't talk about it," I said, "it's gonna drive you crazy."

And so she talked. She finished the cigarette, and then lit a joint, and she talked. Of course, she had been in love with Jack McDaid. She loved his northern furies, she said, his bleak silences, his burly directness. More than anything else, she told me, she loved him because he was still capable of belief. In a way, it didn't matter what he believed as long as he could believe. Nobody in her generation believed in anything anymore, not in God or Marx or the American Way of Life. But Jack McDaid—fifty-two, married, father of four, fallen Catholic, immigrant from Derry, bartender, then bar owner—Jack McDaid believed. And what he believed in was the old dangerous dream of a united Ireland. The dream that had killed Frank Houlihan. The dream that was killing people as we talked.

The words came from her like balled fists, as if death had unraveled her, and she felt she had to explain Sheila Rafferty first, in order to explain the death of Jack McDaid. So she tried to make me understand about growing up in Queens, smart and female and Catholic, imprisoned by nuns and God and parents and scared virginal boys, until she broke out in the sixties and started to reach greedily for everything she'd never had. The story was familiar. Catching up meant running away, joining the guitar army, the flower migration to the West, to Topanga and Haight-Ashbury, to Dylan and the Beatles and the Stones, to lovers, argument, acid, and the inevitable betrayals and disappointments. And then to militant feminism, to all the raised flags of instant revolution, with Jerry and Abbie, the Panthers and Leary and the rest of them crowding the American TV screen, preaching Marxism without Marx, a Left without discipline, justice without sacrifice. After the flowers died, she went back to the East, to the moratoriums in Nixon's

Washington, where tear gas canisters hurtled through the poisoned air and John Mitchell stood on the frigid balcony of the Justice Department smiling his shark's smile; she did all that, with all the others of her generation, and still the blood flowed in Asia. Until she made the wide circle home, through the communes of the Vermont hills, two abortions, her ruptured heart in search of fulfillment.

"Yeah," she said, leaning back, tension ebbing, taut muscles relaxing, "I went home to Queens. My mother was dead by then. My father answered the door and stared at me and let me in, and then walked away while I went to my old room. He didn't say anything. Not then, not after. He just sat in the dark, looking at television, smoking his Camels, and accusing me, with his silence, of killing her. I stayed for a week and then I left for good. The night I left I wandered into McDaid's and met Jack. He fed me. He gave me a job." The joint was out now, reduced to a tiny roach. She reached for my Vantages.

"He was a good-hearted man."

I got up and walked across the sleeping bay to a small refrigerator. I broke out a jug of orange juice, and poured two glasses.

"He was a Provo, wasn't he?" I said, tossing the question over my shoulder, and turning to face her with a glass of juice.

She looked at me with those steady eyes again. "That's none of your business."

"Bullshit," I said. "Someone followed me when I left that place tonight. And I brought Jack McDaid a message from a Provo tonight. From a very big Provo. And that message might have killed him. So don't tell me it's none of my business, Sheila."

I handed her the glass of orange juice. She sipped it without looking at me.

"But maybe you'd better get some sleep before we talk about it," I said.

"I'll never talk about some things, okay? Nothing personal. I just can't."

"Okay."

"His wife must be suffering," she said.

"Did you know her?"

Sheila shrugged. "Only Jack knew her. She was a Catholic. A real Catholic. You know, no birth control. Pray when there's trouble. Suffer in this world so you'll be happy in the next. A real heavy Irish Catholic. Jack understood where she was coming from. She didn't support the . . . what he believed in. She believed in God's will." She hesitated. "But Jack was different. He didn't accept anything."

She gnawed at a knuckle and I thought I knew why she did not want me to take her home. She and Jack McDaid must have shared some small piece of the earth: four walls, a kitchen, some books, a bed, a vision. And toward dawn, he would rise and go to his marriage, to his children and his wife and the chilly breath of God. And tonight, this early morning, she would not even have the continuity of those few hours. She would never have them again. I took her hand.

"You'd better get some sleep," I said.

"I guess."

She tamped out the cigarette, finished the orange juice, and lay back staring at the ceiling. I turned off the light. For awhile, I tried to assemble all the pieces of what had happened, wondering what had been in that lethal envelope, and who the Southerner was, and whether the fire marshals had discovered evidence of a bomb. Sheila Rafferty moved closer to me, sliding one soft leg over mine. I cradled her head in my arm. The pieces of the puzzle were still too jagged and broken, and my brain too weary to form a whole. I dozed, full of obscure dread, and then slept. I woke once and she was gone. I could hear her down below, back on the couch. The sound of grieving whispered through the loft. At least I thought it was grieving. It could have been the wind.

14 It was after ten when I woke up. Sheila was still asleep on the couch, folded into the cushions, covered with a thick eiderdown. I put a full kettle on the stove for coffee, went into the shower and stayed there a long time. When I came out, wrapped in a terrycloth robe, Sheila was sitting at the round oak table near the kitchen window. Her fair skin was blotched and puffy in the hard morning light. She was naked under one of my shirts.

"I made coffee," she said. "I figured that's what the water was for."

She handed me a cup. "Thanks," I said and sipped from the cup. She'd brewed it weaker than I like it. "How are you feeling?"

She glanced into the living room. "I've had better mornings."

"Grab a shower," I said sitting on one of the kitchen stools. "You'll feel cleaner, if not better."

"I might just do that."

She stood up, sipped the coffee, and started past me. She stopped and touched the back of my neck.

"I'm sorry about last night," she said quietly. "What happened here."

"Hey, you said you're not a Catholic anymore. You don't have to load up with the guilt, you know."

"If I'd had to sleep alone, I'd have died."

She removed her hand, but stayed behind me. I turned. She had removed the shirt. She stood with her hands at her side, like a schoolgirl offering herself for inspection. Her face trembled and there were tears welling in her eyes.

"You have to do it again," she said. "You have to."

Blue tracings shimmered beneath the clear white skin. Her breasts moved as she breathed. The tuft of her pubic hair was orange in the sunlight. I held her face in both hands and kissed her.

"I think you should get on with your life," I said.

"There are a lot of things to be done today. By you. By me."

"Please," she said.

She took my hand and placed it between her legs. She was very wet, and shuddered when she brushed herself with my hand.

While she was in the shower, I turned on the radio, finding the all-news AM station. I pulled on checked trousers, black boots, a blue shirt, and learned that in a spring training game against the White Sox, Graig Nettles had injured his ankle, but not seriously. An eight-year-old boy had disappeared while shopping with his mother in the Bronx. The President was drafting another energy bill in Camp David. The usual catalog of chewed newsprint. And then: *Police and fire marshals are investigating an explosion in a Queens bar that killed the owner shortly after closing last night. The explosion was traced to the kitchen, but fire marshals refused comment on the possibility that a bomb had been planted at the rear of the building.* There was no mention of the IRA, or a man from the American South. Or me.

"They never get it right, do they?" Sheila said suddenly.

She was framed by the bathroom door, smelling of soap. Her hair was wet and flat and much darker now. She was wearing the terrycloth robe.

"Well, they don't usually get it right the first time," I said. "When cops refuse to discuss something, it means they know something bad has happened."

"They didn't mention Jack's name, did they?" she said.

"It'll be in the papers," I said. "These news shows are only bulletin operations. They give you a headline and a paragraph, and move on."

"I'd better move on, too. His wife will be in a state."

I asked: "Did she know about you and Jack?"

She snapped a lighter under one of her own Viceroys and looked at me. "Women always know."

"Particularly Irish women."

"Are you Irish?"

"My mother was from County Down," I said. "My father was a Jewish cop from Brownsville. They're both dead."

She turned away from me and started to cry. I put my arms around her, and held her close to me. Then I patted her the way I had patted my daughter a few days earlier, in another country. I hoped she didn't think I was patronizing her; if she did, the hell with her. Smoke drifted acridly from her cigarette. I removed it from her fingers and mashed it out in an ashtray.

"Why don't you tell me what this is all about?" I said. "The only way you'll ever feel better is if we find the people who did it, and make them pay for it."

Her skin felt suddenly chillier. She was silent for a long moment, subtly disengaging herself from me, as if gathering herself for an unpleasant task. Then she began to talk, in a flat monotone. She never looked at me.

Jack McDaid was involved in an arms deal, she said. Not just a few revolvers, or a few Armalites. This was to be the largest shipment of arms in the history of the IRA. The weapons were to be used in a general uprising later in the year, and the order included machine guns, rockets, and heat-seeking missiles for use against British helicopters. That was the way it always seemed to go: you believed first in normal abstractions, in God, or country, or Karl Marx. And then you believed in guns. The guns of liberation. The guns of the dialectic. The guns of heaven. She wasn't sure where they came from, but McDaid's contact was a black man from Harlem. She had never seen the black man, but he had called McDaid several times at her place. McDaid had talked briefly and laconically; she never heard the black man's name. The envelope I'd delivered from Steel probably contained the final instructions on payment and delivery.

"So where are these guns supposed to be shipped from?" I said. I was trying to make my tone casual; it was bad enough that I looked like a cop, I didn't want to sound like one, too.

"Somewhere in New Jersey," she said. "They made a deal with some freighter captain. I didn't really know everything. I didn't want to know everything."

"Why not?"

"The more I knew, the more I might tell if . . . if . . ." She stared off through the window into the gray morning. "I wasn't sure I could resist pain."

She chewed the inside of her lip. I asked her if she could remember a phone number for the black man, or the name of a place where he worked or called from. She looked at me suddenly, her eyes suspicious.

"You're not going to the cops, are you, Briscoe?"

"I should. There's a man dead. Those guns could make a lot of other people dead."

"You *are* going to the cops, aren't you?"

"Give me some reasons why I shouldn't," I said.

She looked at me with blazing eyes. "Reasons? How many reasons do you want? How about the two thousand dead since 1969? How about the thousands—*the millions*—who've died in the last eight hundred years? Do you want the names? How many reasons do you need?"

Her hands moved for another cigarette. I struck a wooden kitchen match. She steadied herself against the counter, her hand beside a bottle of Tanqueray gin.

"I know all about that," I said. "I've read the history and I've been to Belfast."

"Then what the hell's the problem?" she snapped.

"I usually don't care for people who want to murder their way into Utopia."

She slapped me.

"You'd better get dressed," I said. "You'd better get out of here."

15 I thought about Sheila Rafferty all the way to Harlem. She had dressed in silence, and asked only to be dropped off at the Lexington Avenue subway, to go back to her revolution. The guns would get through, she told me. They would get through because they had to get through. They killed Jack McDaid, they could kill her, they could kill fifty more, but the guns would get through. She would do her part. So would all the others. The guns would get through. I had seen a lot of prizefighters talk this way, turning dreams of victory into a chant, forging a kind of primitive verbal armor that would cage up fear. They talked and talked, first to convince themselves, then to convince others, and sometimes it worked and sometimes they walked into a right hand and no words could save them. I wished that Sheila Rafferty had been able to spend a week with my uncle Frank; he could have told her about all the guns that never got through.

But I couldn't go to the police about the guns. When Frank was killed, something had shifted in me; I wasn't joining up with the IRA. I wouldn't help them. I wouldn't act for them. But I wasn't neutral either. I would do nothing to stop an arms shipment from reaching Belfast. But I had other concerns. I wanted to find out who was trying to stop the shipment. The people who were trying to intercept the shipment were the same people who killed Jack McDaid. They were the people who had followed me to Switzerland. And they were probably the people who killed my uncle Frank. I could still operate in that narrow piece of terrain where the blood of families exists. I wanted the killers of my uncle. That was all. I didn't care about resolving eight hundred years of Irish history. I just wanted the people who killed Frank. And I knew I couldn't go to the police about that. They would yawn and call the Feds, and the firearms control people would move in and make some arrests, and everyone else would be on a plane somewhere. There would be a trial, and someone might even go to jail. But nobody would be tried for the death of Frank Houlihan. I would have to deal with those people myself. That's why I was in Harlem. The police weren't the only people who had information about guns.

I parked Red Emma at the bus stop in front of Small's Paradise, locked her, and glowered at two kids standing in a doorway. One of them had a giant radio on his shoulder.

"Touch the car," I said to the bigger one, "and there's six guys inside who'll kill your mother."

"Fuck you," he said. I guess I didn't look too scary.

"I could make you eat that fucking radio if I felt like it," I said. "But I'm late for lunch."

If the car survived the next ten minutes, I'd join the Moral Majority. I laughed, and so did the big kid. The New York ritual was over.

"Anyway," I said, "give me a break."

"Double fuck you," he said.

I feinted him out of position, with a cocked right hand, then turned my back on him and walked into Small's. Jimmy Burnett was at the bar.

Twenty years earlier, he had been one of the brightest of the trumpet players who came after Clifford Brown. He could play fast, he knew the changes, he had a lyric streak and a lovely tone that built on Clifford's legacy and expanded it. He was in the process of making all of that music his own, when he got jammed up with heroin. The cops caught him holding up a drugstore and put him in the slammer for four years. When he got out, his lip was gone and he never played again. He hustled for a few years, becoming the kind of man who could peel an orange with his gloves on, and then picked up a cocaine concession from some of the Cubans who inherited the business from the Italians. He had kicked his own habit years before, and now he was just a large, pleasant, coffee-colored man who liked bourbon and women, and knew everything about the bad side of Harlem. Over the years, I'd done him a few favors.

"Sam Briscoe, I be fucked," he said when I walked

into the wide dark front room. We shook hands. He had the *Daily News* in front of him, open to the racing charts.

"Hello, Jimmy," I said.

"Hey, you lookin' good, man. Except for the hair."

I laughed. "I'll never be as good-lookin' as you, Jimmy."

"Hey, Ralph, bring my man Briscoe sump'n," he said to the bartender. It was twelve-thirty, and the bartender wasn't quite awake yet, sipping coffee from a container and perusing his own *Daily News*. In the big back room a porter swabbed the floor, filling the air with the smell of Clorox and pine. Jimmy nudged me. "Bourbon?"

"Scotch," I said.

He told the bartender to pour some Scotch over some ice.

"I need some help," I said, as the bartender stretched and yawned and walked around the circular bar to find the Scotch bottle.

"Who don't?"

He got up and went to the jukebox and dropped two quarters in the slot. He punched some buttons. The music was very loud. Stanley Turrentine played "Street of Dreams" on his fat Texas-flavored tenor. Jimmy came back and sat beside me on a stool. The juke smothered all other sounds.

"What is it?"

"I need to find a guy."

"Is he hot?"

"I don't think so."

"You gonna put him in the paper?"

"I don't write the column anymore, Jimmy," I said. "You know that."

He sipped his bourbon. "He got a specialty?"

"Guns."

He shook his head and smiled a big Basie-like smile. "Shit."

"A lot of guns," I said. "Let's say if this person exists, he could help certain other persons who could use a lot of guns. He doesn't help them because he agrees with anything they believe. He helps them for money. For a lot of money."

"These other people, they black?"

"Irish."

Turrentine finished. Dinah Washington sang out of the past, "Teach Me Tonight." She made me want to do some serious drinking.

Jimmy lit a Pall Mall.

"Such a dude might exist," he said.

"I'd like to see him."

Jimmy Burnett looked at me without blinking. Then he got up and went outside to the pay phone on the corner.

The picture window covered the length of the living room, and standing alone, twenty-two stories over Riverside Drive, I could see the cold churning waters of the Hudson, the abrupt cliffs of the Palisades across the river, and the charcoal smear of Jersey spreading out to the west. A clock on a factory roof said that it was one-thirty-five. A door clicked softly behind me, and the young woman came back into the room. She was dressed entirely in white, which emphasized her cinnamon skin. Her blouse was sleeveless, her slacks cut tight, and in her white high heels she was more than six feet tall. She looked as if she'd just stepped off the cover of *Essence*.

"Just make yourself comfortable, Mister Briscoe," she said, in a clipped West Indian accent. "Mister Smith will be with you in a moment. Can I freshen that for you?"

"Sure."

She took the Dewar's and soda across the room, trailing a lavender scent, and disappeared through one of four separate doors. The long room had a kind of ghastly glamour, with deep-pile Moroccan rugs on highly polished hard wood floors, and the kind of furniture you only see in *Playboy*. One entire wall was jammed with technology: turntables, speakers, a seven-foot-wide Advent TV screen, a smaller set with three screens for watching all three networks at once, tape decks and labeled shelves full of recordings, from classical to soul, arranged in alphabetical order. These were all encased in custom-built walnut frames, with muted lights discreetly illuminating key switches and functions. On one of the tape decks, a Mozart piano concerto played, as restrained as old money. The rest of the room was just as flamboyantly discreet: Spanish Colonial furniture, traditional lamps, and a deep fireplace piled with logs behind an elegant mesh firescreen. On the wall beside the fireplace a handsomely lit painting glowed with slabs of orange and magenta, a vision of the Mediterranean. It was a Bonnard. The frame was molded wood. There were magazines on various tables: *Vogue, Esquire, Harper's Bazaar, Foreign Affairs, The Nation.* But there were no books.

Above the sideboard there was another Moroccan rug, hung as a tapestry. The rug was flanked by African masks, and there were six African tribal sculptures in the room, including one beautiful Dogon piece standing guard beside the glistening black Yamaha grand piano. On top of the piano was a single framed photograph of Bessie Smith.

The woman came back with the Dewar's and soda.

"It's a beautiful apartment," I said, in my best all-purpose friendly white guy manner.

"Yes," she said coolly and walked to one of the doors. She opened it and was gone. Another door opened.

"So you're Sam Briscoe," the man said. He was tall, and razor thin, dressed in a deep charcoal three-piece suit, pale blue shirt, glossy low-cut boots, wine-colored knit tie. His face was so black that the highlights were blue. I felt I could shave with his trousers.

"And you're Walker Smith," I said, standing to shake his hand. His grip was firm, the skin cool.

"I read you for years," Smith said. "Good stuff. Sorry you stopped. But I guess it takes a lot out of you as you get older."

"Everything does. Now I only work when I need money. Like a stickup man."

"Yes," he said, and smiled thinly. "What can I do for you?"

The woman emerged holding a tumbler of amber liquid that must have been bourbon. He took the drink without acknowledging her, and she drifted away again.

"A man was killed last night in Queens," I said. "His name was McDaid. An hour before he was killed, I handed him an envelope which I had carried from Ireland. Someone tried twice to kill me in the process of delivering it. I think that envelope contained money and shipping instructions. I think they were for you."

Nothing moved in his face. He sipped his bourbon, as calmly as if I'd just told him that the Yankees were losing in the bottom of the fifth.

"What's your angle?" he said.

"I don't like people who try to kill me. I don't like people who kill reasonably decent men like Jack McDaid."

He looked at me now in an amused way.

"It's not that you think this is a good story, is it?" he said. "A story you could sell for a lot of money somewhere? When you run out?"

"No. It's not that."

"Why should I believe you?"

"You have no reason to believe me at all. You just have to take my word for it."

He walked over to the picture window and looked out at the river.

"I'd like to give Jimmy Burnett a good kick in the ass," he said.

"Don't," I said. "He owed me a couple."

"You could be wired. You could be setting me up for something. The goddamn Feds have spent a million trying to get me as it is. And you come walking in here and start talking about trust. *Trust!* Trust is something you eat when you're doing life in Atlanta."

"I have no angle, Walker. I want to find out what's going on, and I want to do it without any cops."

"Why?"

"Because the people involved believe in something."

"Jesus fuckin' Christ. This gets worse."

"When are they supposed to make delivery?"

"I don't know what you're talking about, Briscoe. Delivery of what?"

I pointed a finger at him and squeezed an imaginary trigger.

"You're nuts," he said.

I laughed. "But you have the goods, and you want to get paid. If there's someone around town killing people over those goods, then you could be in trouble. You could get hurt."

"I doubt it."

He walked over to the tape deck. The Mozart had finished. He pulled an album out of one of the neat rows, and placed it on the turntable, flicked some switches, and turned the volume up. It was Charlie Parker.

"Bird, huh?"

"Yeah," he said. "But he was dumb. He died at thirty-four. I'm thirty-three, and I want to live to be eighty."

They were roaring through "A Night in Tunisia," Bird and Dizzy in some lost year after the war, when I was a kid out of Brooklyn and Walker Smith was in diapers.

"What do you want me to do?" he said.

"Go through with the deal. Deliver the guns. Even if the money is short. They're good for it. You'll get it eventually."

"Since when are you negotiating for them?"

"I'm not," I said. "But I know them. They're honorable. You'll get the money."

"That's all you came here for?"

"No," I said. "I want to know where the ship is in Jersey. I might want to be there."

"Why?"

"Because the people I want to get my hands on will probably be there, too," I said. "They'll try to get their hands on the guns themselves."

"Why should I let them do that?"

"Because you won't put the guns on that ship," I said. "You will put those guns on trucks and take them to Baltimore or Boston, and you will put them on another ship and they will go across the ocean and they will be delivered."

"And big brave Sam Briscoe will go to New Jersey and beat up the bad guys."

"Yeah," I said. "With some help from your soldiers."

He burst out laughing. "You're better than Rodney Dangerfield."

"I sing and dance, too."

He leaned back in the leather chair and made a little A-frame with his hands.

"Who are these people, and why won't they just tip the Feds and have all of us locked up?" he said.

"Let me try to make it as simple as possible," I said. "I'm pretty sure they're members of an outfit called the Ulster Volunteer Force. They're a right-wing paramilitary bunch, willing to kill to keep Northern Ireland part of Great Britain. Nobody knows how many of them there are, but we know they're brutal."

"Sounds like the IRA I read about every once in awhile in *The New York Times*."

"Yeah, but there's a difference. The IRA is fighting a war against the British Army. The UVF is fighting Catholics. When the IRA kills a British soldier, the UVF goes out and kills a Catholic. Maybe two. Not an IRA man, necessarily. Any Catholic will do. It's as if a Black Panther had killed a cop in a shootout, and the Ku Klux Klan killed a black man—any black man—in retaliation."

"The Panthers were assholes. Media assholes."

"Some of them were," I said. "Maybe most of them. But killing innocent black people wouldn't be the way to deal with them."

He played with an ivory-handled letter opener. "So you figure this UVF crowd wants those guns for themselves?"

"They could use them."

"You think it's a hijack?"

"Yeah."

He shook his head slowly. Charlie Parker played from beyond the grave. He said, "I don't like this. I don't like it at all. I'm a businessman. I like transactions that are neat.

Clean. No loose ends. This is too sloppy. I could broker that material someplace else."

"That's up to you," I said. "But help me nail these other bastards."

"You're crazy, Briscoe."

"I got company."

16 The Plaza is the dowager who won't die. She was born in 1906 at a cost of twelve million dollars, on the site of the original Plaza Hotel, which cost three million when *it* was built on the site of an old skating rink. The architect was a man named Henry J. Hardenbaugh, who tried to make the new Plaza into a French Renaissance château, the first such château ever to climb eighteen stories into the New York sky. Moving through its marble halls, covering events in the ballrooms, climbing to upper floors in the old hydraulic lifts, investigating its wine cellars and what they used to call the wireless room, walking the mosaic floors in the lobby, or sipping whiskey in the Palm Court, I always felt like a character written by Edith Wharton or Henry James. But on this chilly March afternoon, looking for the southern white man who had carried Plaza stationery to a violent appointment at Mc-Daid's bar in Queens, I felt more like a character out of Sean O'Casey, with some rewriting by Mario Puzo. The shadow of the gunman was upon the land.

I went into the bar off the Oak Room. It was crowded and noisy. Frank Geraghty was behind the stick and smiled when I came in. We grew up in the same neighborhood in Brooklyn and had seen each other in a lot of saloons in the years since we stopped being young. He had another bartender helping with the afternoon crowd.

"A beer, and some real peanuts, Frank," I said.

He grinned. "Salty. Not dry roasted."

"The real stuff."

He turned his broad back to me, walked down the

crowded bar, opened a Heineken, and came back with the
beer and a silver bowl of real honest-to-Jesus salty peanuts.
I told him I needed information.

"About a guest?" he said, bending in close.

"Yeah. A Southerner. I think he was staying here
maybe as late as yesterday. Tall, wiry, bony face. He was
driving a black Buick Regal. I don't have anything else on
him, except that he was outside McDaid's bar in Queens last
night when it blew up."

Frank's face darkened. He looked at the crowd at the
bar, then back at me.

"The hotel's full, Sam. That's more than two thousand
people here. Some of them are sleeping in closets."

"Do you have a list of events back there? Meetings,
conventions, that kind of thing?"

He came back with a mimeographed sheet with a Plaza
logo, and while he served other customers, I ran down the
list. Society of Magazine Publishers. International Shoe
Manufacturers' Guild. Sansui Ltd. of Tokyo. The National
Petroleum Suppliers. I took out a pen and circled one group.
The Church of Christ the Leader. CCL. The initials doodled
on that sheet of stationery.

"Try this group," I said. "The house dick would know
what floor they're on. Maybe a maid—"

Frank whispered: "What's this about, Sam?"

"Ireland," I said.

"Really?"

He murmured something to the other bartender and
went out a small back door. A man wearing a shoe
manufacturer's badge was drunk at the end of the crowded
bar and kept yelling that New York was a sewer, New York
was a ripoff. He must have had a heavy lunch. At a corner
table two ladies with blue-rinsed hair sipped colored drinks
in tiny glasses. I wondered what the hotel had been like that
first day, years ago, when Mr. and Mrs. Alfred Gwynne
Vanderbilt were the first guests to sign the register, and the
Goulds and the Harrimans and "Bet-A-Million" Gates
followed them through the doors, all of them brimming with

the confidence that the world they had made would last forever.

It didn't.

Everything went through those doors in the years that followed: debutantes and busted royalty, swindlers and statesmen, home run hitters and rock n' rollers. Valentino stayed there, and Caruso, and Scott Fitzgerald got drunk in the Grill one night and went outside and dived into the fountain. Even a piece of my history belonged to the Plaza. The night we got married, Elaine and I made love in a suite on the fourteenth floor and then had brandy in the Palm Court. Everything changes. Nothing lasts. But, I knew there were still young people sitting over brandy out there in the Palm Court, with their whole lives laid out before them. Someone should be out there, warning them about the reefs in the peacock sea. Someone who wasn't me.

Frank Geraghty came back. His face told me he had found what he had gone to find. "Try this," he said, slipping me a piece of paper. Then he went down the bar to deal with the drunk, who had just announced loudly that New York sucked.

There was one name on the plain piece of paper. Manning. And a room number—1209.

Frank suggested to the drunk that he should go upstairs and take a nap. The drunk said he wasn't tired. Frank leaned in and said something in his ear. The drunk blinked and then slowly gathered his change and left. Frank came back down the bar.

"Go out in the lobby and look for the bellhop with the gold pin in his jacket," Frank said. "He'll take you up there. There's nobody in the room. The bellhop thinks you're a cop."

"Thanks, Frank."

"Don't steal anything up there, for Christ's sake."

"I won't. And, Frank?"

"Yes?"

"What'd you tell the drunk?"

"I told him if he didn't sleep upstairs, he'd sleep in the fuckin' morgue."

He laughed in a mirthless way and went down to serve two more men with their names pasted to their lapels, and their heads full of shoes.

The bellhop waited in the hall. I closed the door behind me. R. Manning had rented a small suite: a sitting room and a bedroom. The housekeepers had been through already, cleaning and straightening, so it was difficult to learn much about his habits. A dark blue blazer with cheap brass buttons was hanging in the closet, with gray trousers on a separate hanger. A pair of black loafers, scuffed, as if from running, was on the floor. In the bottom of the dresser drawer there were some dirty clothes. Jockey shorts. Socks. And a shirt with brick-colored blotches on the front that could have been blood. It might have been the shirt he was wearing when I cracked him, but I didn't really remember what he was wearing the night before. The brand on the shirt in the drawer was Arrow. Nothing fancy. There were stencils from a laundry over the brand label. If I were a cop, these details would mean something. But I wasn't a cop, and they didn't.

I found something more useful on the table beside the bed. A stack of pamphlets on top of a book. The book was *The Orange State* by Michael Farrell. It was one of the best books on Northern Ireland, written by an Irish Marxist, but crammed with reliable facts and figures. Michael Farrell had been in the group called People's Democracy in the early sixties when civil rights were the focus of the Irish protests; in those days the educated Irish liberals believed that violence was an anachronism. Michael Farrell, in that time, agreed. He was a teacher at Queens University, Belfast, while Steel was there as a student. Certainly they must have known each other. R. Manning was researching the enemy with some of the best available material. I glanced through the book; the most theoretical passages were highlighted with a yellow felt pen. None of the aching history, none of the facts, none of the hard figures had been marked at all.

The pamphlets were all published by the Church of

Christ the Leader, and they were, in their way, wonderful. They had titles like "Christ, Marx, and Water Pollution" and "The Soviets and Price Controls" and "The Thirteenth Tribe of Israel and the Oil Crisis." None was marked with the yellow pen. I wrote down the address of the Church of Christ the Leader, in Fort Lee, New Jersey. Right across the river. And then I left, slipped the bellhop a twenty, and went into the darkening afternoon.

Charlie Kelly was at a table next to the side door at P. J. Clarke's. Almost everybody I knew was certain to be found in bars, even at four in the afternoon. I suppose it was because I had reached that time in life when none of my friends were married any longer. People who live alone eat out, and when they finish eating out, they drink out. Sometimes they drink out before they eat out. Or maybe it was just a sign that my only friends were cops, reporters, bartenders, and bums. Charlie Kelly was a cop, and a good one.

"Hey, Hebe," he said as I came in, and waved a hamburger at an empty chair. "Siddown."

"Hello, Charlie."

His blue eyes were slightly out of focus; he was either depressed, distracted, or hungover. He looked at me with his most serious expression.

"What do you know about biology?" he said.

"I could look it up under "B" in the *Encyclopedia Brittanica*," I laughed. "Why?"

"That kid of mine," he said. "He calls me about genes and chromosomes, and asks me to explain, and I don't know a goddamned thing about any of it. And I feel like a goddamned failure all over again. Rape and mayhem and safecracking I know. Genes and chromosomes I don't know."

For eleven months, Charlie Kelly had been married to a Rockette, and he had been divorced now for at least eleven years. His ex-wife was a beautiful woman, but I was certain she didn't know any more about the theory of genes and chromosomes than Charlie did.

"I know a biology professor at Columbia," I said. "Maybe she can find a tutor for the kid. I could give her a call."

"Do that for me, will you, Briscoe?"

"Sure," I said. "I want you to do something for me, too."

"Aw, shit, Sam. Not more trouble."

"Nothing else."

I told him I wanted to check out one R. Manning, associated with the Church of Christ the Leader, in Fort Lee, New Jersey. I gave him Manning's room number at the Plaza and assured him there must be fresh prints in the room. The waiter came over, and I ordered a burger and a beer.

"How fast do you need all this?" Charlie Kelly said wearily, looking at his watch.

"Tonight, if you can do it."

"Is this another one of your goddamned capers, Sam? If it is, you better tell me the rest, so we don't end up with dead guys."

"I don't know what it's all about yet," I said. I hesitated, wondering if I would hurt more people if I told him what I knew. Then: "The guy might have something to do with the bomb that blew up a joint called McDaid's in Woodside last night."

The father left his face as it hardened into cop. "That means there's one dead guy already."

"Yeah."

He got up and went to the pay phone. The front bar was filled with stockbrokers and advertising men trying to be *macho*. I liked the back and hated the front of Clarke's, but on either side of the shadow line, they still made the best hamburger in Christendom. I ate my hamburger while Charlie worked the pay phone and the stockbrokers argued about the Rangers and the Islanders. I tried to remember when I'd ever heard a black man talk about hockey, and my eyes drifted to the Irish flags behind the bar, the pictures of Patrick Pearse and Michael Collins and other martyrs of old

Irish wars. Frank Sinatra was singing "You Make Me Feel So Young" on the jukebox. Charlie came back.

"Any luck?"

"They're working on it. You'll have to check me in a couple of hours. You marching in the parade?"

"No," I said. "I gave it up when I was thirteen. On St. Patrick's Day I'm Jewish. The Irish half of me is too embarrassed."

"Puerto Rico is the perfect place for St. Patrick's Day," he agreed. "I wish they would make singing "Danny Boy" a felony, so I could lock up most of the bastards that come in here."

"If they do," I said, "let me know. I'll make a few citizen's arrests myself."

I got up and went to the phone and called my service. There had been two hangups. An editor had called to say the piece was fine, and would be in the bulldog edition tonight. And there was a message from Sheila: "Meet me in the Green Derby at six." That was all. The woman from the answering service laughed when she gave me that one. Only two days until St. Patrick's Day. Beautiful. But the two hangups made me a little edgy.

"I hope you're getting laid tonight," Charlie Kelly said when I came back to the table.

"Not tonight," I said.

"It's been so long since I got laid, I forget what you're supposed to do."

"Concentrate," I said. "You'll remember. Just don't get married again to find out. You gonna be here?"

"No, I thought I'd go home and read some biology."

"I'll call you in a couple of hours."

17 One more bar. I was starting to feel like Ulysses in Nighttown. I parked Red Emma on Second Avenue, a block north of the Green Derby. The place was Real Irish, not "Danny Boy" Irish. The bartenders were Irish and the waitresses were Irish and the customers were Irish. Irish from Ireland, not New Jersey.

There were a lot of customers. They were packed against the bar, and four bartenders were filling their glasses, and the Dubliners were singing from the jukebox, and there were collection boxes for the prisoners in Long Kesh, and "Smash Internment" posters and "To Hell With the Queen" posters, and another poster asking them to picket the Big Four, who, a year before, had issued a collective statement on St. Patrick's Day condemning the violence of the IRA and asking Irish-Americans to end their support of "terrorism." This statement had received glowing support on the editorial pages of the newspapers of the United States and created a storm of rage among supporters of the IRA. The Big Four apparently had decided that they needed those editorial pages more than they needed whatever Irish votes still existed on an issue that so many had left behind when they came to America. And as I peered through the smoke, I could see what the customers of all the Green Derbies of New York were being asked to picket. A dinner. A dinner sponsored by the American-Irish Historical Society, on the night before St. Patrick's Day.

An idea began to form in my mind, indistinct and obscure but becoming clearer, like a photograph in a tray of developer. The dinner was scheduled for the Grand Ballroom of the Plaza Hotel.

I looked around and there was no sign of Sheila. I reached through the crowd and ordered a beer. The bartender reacted quickly, producing a beer and change of a five in one fluid motion, and moved on. The music was very loud. I could hear a Cork accent arguing with a Mayo accent. Some of the drinkers mentioned the names of the Big Four. Others discussed some obscure hurling match. Two were arguing the concept of the Virgin Birth.

Then Sheila touched my elbow.

"You came," she said.

"Yeah."

A fine web of muscles moved in her jaw before she spoke. She had changed her clothes and was wearing a dark blue turtleneck under a gray tweed jacket. Her pressed denims and high heels made her look very crisp and businesslike.

"Well?" I said.

"Steel's in town," she said, and moved away from me through the bar crowd, heading for a narrow passageway at the far end of the saloon. I put the beer on a table and followed her. She wasn't in the kitchen, and I didn't try the restrooms. There was another door at the end of the passageway. I opened it, and stepped into a narrow alley.

I saw some garbage cans, and then there was a swift movement on my left. A jagged red scribble went through my eyes, and then there was blackness.

18 I opened my eyes and saw nothing. I closed them, and saw a red film with amorphous shapes swimming in the redness. I tried again. This time I saw Jimmy McLarnin, with his hands up, and a choirboy smile on his face, wearing the championship belt of the thirties. All in faded sepia.

I closed them again, and tried to move. The hurt shifted from the base of my skull to my back. I tried my hands; they also wouldn't move.

When I opened my eyes again, the picture of McLarnin was joined by framed photographs of Barney Ross and Floyd Patterson and Sugar Ray Robinson. There was a sign saying No Smoking and two chairs. There were human legs in each of the chairs, and a pair of high heels jutted out of one pair of denims. There was a bottom of a desk. There was a wastebasket. There was a baseball bat in a corner, and a TV set on a small table. I tried to turn to see who the legs belonged to, and then someone nudged me with a foot, and I turned over on my back. Sheila was staring down at me. A guy was sitting in the chair beside her.

"I'm sorry, Sam," she said.

"So am I," I said. My voice was a croak, and I ran my tongue over the roof of my mouth, trying to moisten the blood-caked surface.

"You know some things that could be dangerous." A pause. "To our people."

I tried to laugh; it didn't come, but I hoped she got the idea. "You're not trying to tell me I know too much, are you?"

"Something like that."

"Jesus."

"What's so funny?"

"Nothing. It's not funny at all. Except that Fu Manchu used the line a lot more convincingly than you do."

She turned away, her eyes wandering to the baby face of Jimmy McLarnin, staring out at all of us from the thirties. She spoke softly: "There was some talk about killing you. I talked them out of it."

"Ah, counsel for the defense."

"Don't be a wise guy, Briscoe," she said curtly. "I could talk them back into it."

"For what? I don't get any of this."

"We have something important that we must do," she said in a blank ritualized voice. "But you're a wild card. You stumbled into something, and now you're in the way. So we'll have to keep you out of the way."

"And then what?" I said. "You have dimbrain here shove me in the river?"

"We're waiting for orders."

"Then order me a ham on rye, no mayo, pickle on the side."

Her lip curled in contempt; I wasn't acting with

sufficient reverence for the Holy Cause, whatever the hell it was, and this poor little girl could never allow humor into the heart because then the cause and everything connected to it would crumble away. She was obviously a woman who had seen a lot of things crumble away, and wasn't going to let it happen again.

"You talk too much, Briscoe."

"That's what happens when you live alone," I said.

I shifted my weight. My feet were tied with a rope with handles on it. A skip rope. My hands and upper arms were lashed together behind me. And then I suddenly realized exactly where I was. I was in a gym. And not just any gym. I was in the Gramercy Gym on Fourteenth Street. I was in the office where Cus D'Amato once lived, when he was managing Floyd Patterson and Jose Torres and a lot of other fighters. Cus had been gone a long time, but the gym was still there, and I was in it now, tied up on the floor. I looked at the man in the chair next to Sheila, and now I knew him, too.

"Hello, Barney," I said.

"Where do you know him from?" Sheila said, suddenly alarmed. She looked from me to the big man in the chair beside her.

"I knew Barney Mullins when he was a fighter," I said. "He was a big heavyweight, off the boat from Ireland, and they put him in the Golden Gloves. Right out of this gym. Everybody was looking for a white heavyweight in those days. And an Irish heavyweight, forget it. *He* could have become a millionaire."

"Shut up," Barney said.

"So there was Barney Mullins, and a big son of a bitch he was," I said. "Well, he won the sub-novice Golden Gloves championship that first year. But, basically, he did it by outhugging the other stiffs. Oh, he could punch, all right. It's just that he had a heart the size of a flea's prick."

"Enough of your gub," Barney said, and stood up, looking over me.

"Sit down, Barney," Sheila said. He ignored her.

I kept talking. "The other managers looked at Barney,

and the way he behaved, and they learned that if you pressed him, he became a pacifist. He would look for exit signs. He would look for help. Since there's no help in a ring, Barney didn't last. Cus D'Amato showed him how to defend himself, but it wasn't enough. So Cus turned him pro, got him to sign a five-year contract, let him fight twice, and then retired him. Barney left the gym and went to work in saloons. In saloons you can fight drunks. You can fight bullshit artists. You just never fight fighters."

"I don't have to take this," Barney said. His flat seamed face was flushed with anger.

"So I figure it was you who blindsided me, Barney," I said. "That's your basic act."

He came over fast and kicked me in the ribs. I could feel the bile move up to meet the dried blood in my throat. I was cut inside the mouth somewhere. Or the nose was gone again.

"Barney, wait outside!" Sheila said sharply. "Better yet, get some water from the fountain out there."

Barney stood up, and then walked heavily away on his big feet, muttering bitterly. I tried to laugh.

"What the hell did you take me *here* for?" I said.

"Barney owns this place," she said. "He manages boxers."

This time I got the laugh out.

"Perfect," I said. "Them who can, do. Them who can't, manage."

Barney came back with a glass of water. Sheila squatted beside me and pressed the glass to my lips. I swallowed some, rinsed my mouth, turned aside, and spat it out. It was pink.

"Is it my mouth or my nose?" I said.

"Your nose."

"Jesus, Barney, you're punching better now than you did twenty years ago."

"Do me a favor, Briscoe?" Sheila said. "Stop talking, okay? You're only making things worse."

"I'll tell you what," I said. "Take that skip rope off my feet and let me sit up, and I'll stop breaking balls."

She looked at me coldly. Then: "Take it off, Barney."

"I'd like to make him eat it."

"He's not going anywhere. Not for twenty-four hours, at least."

Barney started opening the knots in the skip rope, breathing heavily from the exertion.

"Don't you think the fighters are going to be a little surprised tomorrow," I said, "to see a guy tied up in the office?"

"The gym is closed for two days," he said. "It's an Irish gym now. We close for St. Patrick's."

"You mean you found an Irish heavyweight, Barney? Someone who can do what you didn't have the heart to do?"

"Shut up," Sheila said. "Barney, get him some more water."

My legs were free now, and I braced myself against a wall and stood up. I did some squats to get the blood moving, and then strolled over to a mirror above the sink, with my hands and arms still tied behind my back. A door next to the sink led to the lavatory. Through another door, I could see the familiar silhouettes of the gym: the black lines of the ring ropes, the heavy bags hanging against the glow of the big windows, and some of the lights of Fourteenth Street leaking onto the gym floor. The fluorescents hummed in the office, but everything else was dark.

"It's my nose, all right," I said. There was a swelling at the bridge and caked blood on my upper lip. He had hit me a perfect sucker punch. "Ah, well. It's probably an improvement."

Barney walked in with another glass of tepid water. Sheila held it to my lips, and I sipped. I rinsed my mouth and spat a pink blob into the sink. She turned on the tap. Barney snorted. I heard a door open, out in the gym, the heavy iron door that I knew led to two long flights of stairs and the street.

"There's Sandy," Barney said.

"No more names, for God's sake," Sheila said.

"He'll tell no one," Barney said heavily, looking at me. I knew he was packing a gun now; those big soft ones get much braver when they're carrying iron. "He'll never say a bloody word."

A thin young man appeared in the doorway. His hair was a sandy dark blond, his face freckled, his neck thin, his hands jammed into the pockets of a tweed jacket. He had cold gray eyes and not much chin. He was about twenty.

"Yo, Sandy, come join the party," I said. "We're celebrating my kidnapping."

He looked surprised.

"It doesn't matter," Sheila said. "He knows me, too, and he knows Barney."

That's when I started to feel afraid. They were acting like amateurs. Amateurs always talk too much. And in all the crafts of the world, amateurs were dangerous, particularly in the craft of kidnapping.

"I don't like this," Sandy said, in a West Belfast accent. "Nobody told me he'd know who we are."

"It doesn't matter," she said again. "He can't do anything while he's here, and by the time he leaves, we'll have finished the assignment."

Sandy looked even more dubious now. He stared at me for a long beat, and then took off his jacket. There was a fat Colt .45-automatic in a holster on his hip. The gun was too big for him. He sighed and said, "Well, I guess maybe it doesn't matter."

"No," Sheila said. "It doesn't matter. It won't matter until it's over."

And then I suddenly understood what they might be planning to do. The Plaza. They were going to kill the Big Four at the Plaza. It didn't make much sense, but I knew that's what it was. Certainly it made no sense politically. If they killed a couple of Senators, the Speaker, a Governor, they'd never get another penny from their supporters in the United States; the public outrage could even destroy the IRA in Northern Ireland. But maybe they thought that a great spectacular was what they needed to set off the general rising. The rising that would be armed with those guns from a New Jersey port. Revolutionaries usually have an unreal idea of the way their actions are perceived by the outside world, and these amateur revolutionaries were probably no different from the others. Maybe they thought that killing the Big Four would be viewed as a symbol of their power to strike anywhere and at anyone. In one mighty blow, they could acquire an image of power and ruthlessness, forcing the world to take them seriously. I could picture Sheila and Barney and this dumb kid watching the triumphant explosion. I could see them in my imaginary picture, but I still couldn't see Steel.

"Watch him carefully, Sandy," Sheila said abruptly, glancing at her watch. "He's not stupid."

"Aye."

"If he tries anything," Barney said, "shoot him."

19 Without another word they went out, slamming the gym door behind them. I was alone with young Sandy. He turned on the TV set, and we watched Cary Grant in *Bringing Up Baby*. It was a good movie, but I didn't pay much attention. My hands hurt from the ropes. I tried to think. There were too many loose ends for any simple theory. Who was R. Manning, and how did he fit into this? He was staying at the Plaza. I knew that for sure. Sheila said she was on the side of the IRA but R. Manning certainly wasn't. Maybe Sheila wasn't IRA at all. Maybe she helped R. Manning blow up McDaid's and then set me up. But why didn't she just kill me? She had me in the loft. She could have cut my throat while I slept. But she didn't do that. She had revealed a lot of herself to me that night. It couldn't all have been an act. But what about Steel? Why would Steel agree to a crackpot stunt like killing the Big Four? Was he really in New York? Did he know what this trio of amateurs was doing? It was all too much for the bruised and broken synapses in my skull. I looked at Sandy.

He was sitting against a wall, the automatic in front of him on the floor. His brain was wrapped in Cary Grant. I stretched my legs on the old worn couch, and realized that I

97

couldn't feel anything in my fingers anymore. Barney Mullins had tied the ropes tightly. I remembered Barney cowering in a corner twenty years ago, while some tough kid fresh out of the Salem Crescent Club unloaded the combinations, every one of the punches hurting Barney and blotching his white skin until the referee stepped in and saved Barney for future service to the IRA. Maybe this was his way of redeeming his life. On the other hand, he could be just another example of Charlie Kelly's Law—the bigger the dog, the bigger the gun.

I began to think about the immediate problem. I was trapped in a place I might never leave alive. Amateurs can never think of anything to do with witnesses except kill them. Professionals only kill the people they have to kill, which is why they almost never pull kidnappings. But this boy Sandy was an amateur. As a boy, he would gladly kill me if he were asked. It would take one phone call. Barney might kill me without being asked. The first thing I had to do was get out of the gym.

"Like the movie?" I said to Sandy, in my best all-American asshole manner.

"Good. Good crack."

"Cary Grant's an Englishman, you know."

"Is he?"

"Sure. His real name's Archie Leach."

"Go away out of that," he protested.

"You could look it up."

He blinked at me, stared back at the movie, then to me again. "Well, maybe you're right. It's a funny accent."

"What do you think Steel would say if he knew you were enjoying an Englishman in a movie?"

His eyes narrowed. "What do you mean?"

"Ask Steel," I said. "Sheila says he's in New York."

"What do you know about Commander Steel?" he said.

"He's a friend of mine."

He spit against the wall.

"Well, that's a hape of shite," he said.

He was right about that.

"I was with him three days ago," I said, weaving a few facts into the lie. "In the International Hotel in Belfast. I wrote a story about him for the *Daily News*. It'll be on the stands tonight."

He squinted again. "Commander Steel never gives interviews. Why would he talk to you?"

"Because I'm a goddamned good reporter," I said. "Because he knew I'd give him a fair shake. Because my uncle Frank was in the IRA before you were born, and before Steel was born, and he asked Steel to talk to me." I paused. "And when it was over, my uncle Frank—Frank Houlihan—got his throat cut. Go ahead. Call Belfast and check. There's a phone right there on the wall."

He ignored the TV set completely now. He picked up the gun and fiddled with it as if it were some monstrous new toy he'd found under a Christmas tree. I sat up slowly on the edge of the couch. He whipped around with the gun on me.

"Relax," I said quietly.

"Don't move."

"A man can piss, can't he?"

He looked behind him at the narrow door to the lavatory. His face was dubious, but he lowered the gun.

"You don't look like one of us," he said.

"You mean I don't look Catholic?"

"Aye."

"Well, neither did Jesus Christ, boy," I said. "He was just a nice Jewish carpenter."

He blinked. That always got these dumb Catholic kids. If Jesus was Jewish, what other heresies could be abroad in the land? I talked faster then, repeating what Steel had told me. The struggle in Northern Ireland was about class, I said, not religion. The IRA was fighting for Ireland, not Catholicism. The British ruling class had spent centuries setting the Catholic and Protestant working people against each other for their own benefit, and the IRA was determined to drive them out of Ireland once and for all. Sandy listened intently; he obviously had heard some of these words before, even if he hadn't quite understood them. He listened, and now I really did have to piss.

"If Steel is really in New York," I said, "then call him. Go ahead. Call him, or call Belfast. But for Christ's sake, let me piss, will you?"

He sighed and stood up, the gun in his right hand, hanging at his side. He looked into the narrow lavatory. A bowl and sink, and a pile of *Penthouse* magazines.

"Have your piss."

I stood up.

"I have a slight problem," I said.

He looked at me dimly.

"I can't unzipper my fly with my foot."

He smiled nervously, and lit a Winston with a Bic lighter. Then he seemed embarrassed; he might even have blushed, although his skin color wasn't clear under the humming fluorescent lights.

"Go ahead," I said. "Unzipper it."

"But then—"

"Yeah," I said. "You'll have to whip out my prick."

Now he really did blush. I was next to him, trying to get past him to the lavatory.

"It's all right with me," I said, "and I'm sure it's okay with God. Don't think of it as a venial sin. Think of it as a corporal work of mercy."

He laughed nervously, put the gun on the chair, and unzippered my fly. He fumbled with my shorts, and took out my cock, and then I slammed him against the frame of the door. I slammed him again, as hard as I could, jamming his spine against the frame, and then I butted him in the teeth. He fell away, and I stepped back and kicked a field goal with his head. He fell in a shambling pile, wedged against the wall and the bowl.

Then I turned around and kicked the gun away. It fell behind the couch. I went out to the gym. The lock was high on the door; I turned around, bending forward to get my hands up higher. Sandy groaned. I could see him beginning to move. The lock slipped in my sweaty hands. The numb fingers were as clumsy as a glove full of nickels. I seemed to be there for twenty minutes. A half hour. The useless fingers working the lock. Then Sandy was standing, blood streaming from his nose, making jerky sounds as he came out of the john. He looked for the gun. Then he picked up a baseball bat.

He came for me.

I lowered my head and charged.

He swung.

The bat whipped through the air over my head, and I smashed into his belly with my head, driving him back against a huge mirror used for shadow boxing. The mirror splintered into a thousand pieces. I stomped and kicked and stomped some more, and left him bleeding and ruined on a bed of fractured glass.

I came out onto Fourteenth Street. Three Puerto Ricans were standing under the marquee of the Academy of Music. They looked up. Here came me—blood on my face, hands tied behind my back, and my cock hanging out.

"*Mira, hombres, ayúdame!*" I yelled.

"Hey, man—"

"Some fags from the park kidnapped me. Tied me up. Went after my cock. I just escaped."

"*Carajo*," the tallest one said. He reached into his pocket, whipped out a switchblade, pressed a button. A large blade popped out. The skip rope fell to the sidewalk with a clatter of handles.

"Where are them motherfuckas?" one of them said.

"Up there," I said. "In the gym."

"Le's go kick their fuckin' ass, man," the big one said. "Fuckin' fags ruinin' the neighborhood, man."

I rubbed my wrists, but felt nothing.

"New York is goin' to the fuckin' *dogs*, man," the big one said.

"Happy St. Patrick's Day," I said, and zippered my fly and headed for Third Avenue. Around the corner, in a parking lot, I unzippered again. There have been few moments of my life to equal that bliss.

20 I went into the Blarney Stone three blocks away. The clock over the bar told me it was ten after one. There were four stewbums at the bar, watching John Wayne destroy the Japanese army at Iwo Jima. He looked very convincing for a man who sat out the war at Republic Pictures. I put a dollar on the bar and asked for a Coke. I drank it down, and ordered another. The bartender held the coke, waiting to see another dollar. I put a five on the bar and he opened the Coke. The stewbums stirred at the sound of coins. I picked up the change and went down to the pay phone. I called Charlie Kelly at Clarke's.

"He and Lavezzo went out to eat," the Clarke's bartender said. Danny Lavezzo owned the place. "They get tired of hamburgers."

"Thanks," I said. "When Charlie comes back, tell him Briscoe called."

My voice sounded vacant and distant. I tried to put another dime in the slot and completely missed the phone. My fingers seemed made of sponge. On the third attempt, I somehow persuaded the dime to fall into the little hole. I dialed Marta Torres. She picked up and said hello in a drowsy voice.

"It's me," I said.

"Well, that's news," she said. "Briscoe calls in at last."

"Marta, I have to stay there tonight," I said, my voice still coming from a long way away.

"Sorry, bright boy. I'm booked."

"I'm in a jam," I said. "I can't go home. I've been hurt."

She sighed. "Goddamn you, Sam. Every time I think I've got you out of my system, you show up again, and you're always *bleeding*."

I tried to laugh, but the nausea was moving through me like gas. I thought I was going to vomit. I went very still.

"I know," I said slowly. "I know. It's all true. I'm careless. I'm thoughtless. I'm a pain in the ass." I pulled away from the phone and fought for control. "But I, uh—"

"Come on up," she said.

"You said you were booked."

"I am," she said. "I'm trying for the fourth time to get through the first thirty pages of *Garp*. I guess I'll never read that goddamned book."

"I'll be there in ten minutes."

"Try not to throw up in my lobby," she said. "I have enough trouble with management just being a Puerto Rican."

I went outside and hailed a yellow cab. Marta Torres was a lawyer for one of the few honest anti-poverty agencies. After three years of helping put landlords in jail, the job was almost over; but with the Feds cutting all such budgets, the landlords would be safer now and people like Marta Torres would move on. I knew she would hang in until the very end; she never quit on anything important in her life. She was tall and beautiful, with high cheekbones, copper-colored skin, lustrous black hair; she had worked as a model to pay her way through school, and when she graduated from Columbia Law she never stood in front of a camera again. A brilliant student, she worked briefly for one of the old-line Protestant law ghettoes on Wall Street after graduating, but she didn't stay long. She didn't like defending people she knew were criminals. For four years now, she had been defending the poor. Once, she had saved my life. She also made me laugh. I liked her more than anyone I knew. But I didn't know what to do about it.

"Well, if it isn't Mister Death On a Soda Cracker of 1959," she said, answering the door in a plaid bathrobe. I smiled, or tried to, and walked in. She locked two locks behind me. I looked around. The snow in the Paul Davis poster for *The Cherry Orchard* began to move. So did the walls. "First stop is the shower," she said. "I'll have the clothes burned. You smell like Nixon's soul."

"I don't know if I can manage a shower, unless you get in with me and hold me up."

"I'm not taking a shower with you in this condition," she said. She was holding me under the arm now. The lights were muted. She moved me toward the bedroom. On the bed, there really was a copy of *The World According to Garp*. I sat on the edge of the bed. "Holy God, look at that nose."

"Is the bathtub working?" I said.

"Better than you are," she said. I undressed while she ran the bath, and then she came back and helped me get up. She led me into the bathroom. The tiles were cold under my feet. I slipped into the scalding hot bath. I jumped, moaned, then settled. The womb.

"You want to tell me what this is all about?" she said. I told her most of it, but not all. I left out what had happened with Sheila in the loft. She shook her head.

"Well, it seems all very simple to me," she said. "You call up the FBI, and tell them what you think is going on. They'll go to the Plaza and scan it. If necessary, they'll evacuate the place. And then you can read about it in the papers, *cuate*. But you don't get involved anymore than you are involved right now."

"I wish it was that simple."

I tried to explain my complicated feelings about the IRA. I told her what had happened to my uncle Frank, and that I didn't like getting slugged, slapped around, tied up. I told her I had to find out whether the IRA arms shipment was connected to the IRA plan to blow up the Plaza. I didn't mind the gun deal, because I thought the IRA was fighting a war, and soldiers had to get guns wherever they could get them. But I didn't like the Plaza job. If there *was* a Plaza job. She listened quietly. She ran more hot water into the tub. Then I was nauseated again. She left the bathroom and came back with a shot of Scotch. I sipped it, hating the smell, but shuddering nicely to the burning feeling as it went down; it was as if the Scotch were cutting through whatever was blocked inside me.

"What do you want me to do?" she said.

"Nothing," I said.

"Stop, Sam," she said. "If you won't call the Feds,

then this thing is gonna get away from you. You can't handle it alone."

"I know."

"So?"

I asked her to keep trying Charlie Kelly until she found him. Find out what he had discovered about R. Manning. Then she could go down to the *Daily News* and use their morgue. Look up an outfit called Church of Christ the Leader. Look up R. Manning. Look up any other names that Charlie had discovered. Maybe if I knew the cast, I could think about what to do. R. Manning didn't seem part of the IRA, and if he wasn't, I wanted to know what he was a part of. She made some notes. Then she helped me out of the tub, and started drying me off with a large rough towel.

"Easy there," I said.

"Shut up and enjoy it," she said.

"I wish I could."

"So do I."

In my dream a giant condor came out of the sea and perched above me on the Brooklyn Bridge. I began to run and the bird dived, and my legs wouldn't move, and I tried to jump off the bridge into the black waters below, and then the condor swooped and came at me. In another dream, I was a boy again, and a giant wave was rolling at the beach of Coney Island and we were trying to run and I was calling for my father and my father wasn't there. There were other dreams, too—turbulent with dread, and things beyond control. In my life, I'd had a lot of dreams like that.

When I woke up, it was afternoon. Marta was gone and there was a file folder on the night table beside the phone. A note was clipped to the front.

Sam:

If I charged you by the hour (which I should) you would owe me about two thousand dollars. Here's everything I could find. Charlie Kelly is worried about you. So am I. So don't go anywhere without letting us know. My car keys are on the table in the kitchen; and the car's in space E-4 in the basement garage. I took Red Emma to work. Nobody you know will be looking for her in *El* Bronx.

You sure looked cute in the tub, ugly one.

Love,

M

The first sheet was notes from her conversation with Charlie Kelly. He had checked out R. Manning. The facts were Charlie's; the words came from Marta:

"Richard Manning, forty-one years old. Born in Spartanburg, South Carolina. His yellow sheet was opened at age fifteen. Stolen car, assault with intent. He did some time. When he came out, became a dealer working truck stops: selling pills, ups, downs, reds, blues, some coke, some heroin. Also worked for a bootlegger. Then at age twenty-one, he gets picked up in Baltimore for killing a guy with a pipe in a poolroom. He did six years for manslaughter. It would have been more, except the dead man was black. Then he goes back to South Carolina, gets tied up with the White Citizens Council and the Klan. Arrested twice for beating up Freedom Riders; released each time for lack of evidence. Major suspect in killing of white woman, civil rights worker, in Mississippi, 1966. Jury won't convict. Suddenly: praise God! He gets his little white self borned again."

I sat up on the edge of the bed, and found a cigarette. The smoke tasted sour.

"He was converted into . . . the Church of Christ the Leader," the memo said. "This is a corporation run by a father and son TV preacher act (see attached stuff from the *News* morgue). Manning is now a deacon in the church, which is located right across the river in Fort Lee, New Jersey. Keep your ass in Manhattan, brother."

She had made Xerox copies of a lot of material from the *Daily News* morgue, and thrown in some pictures from the photo file. Some of the clips were very dark; the originals must have been yellow from age. I put out the cigarette and lay back and read the story told by the clips. It was a very American story.

The father was named Martin Parsons. The son was Martin Junior. They had been part of the holy alliance of God and money since before Jerry Falwell knew how to spell moral. Martin Parsons Senior was born in Rolling Fork, Iowa, in 1896. His father sold farm implements. Martin went to public schools in Iowa, and all through high school helped in his father's business—after school, on weekends, during vacations—there wasn't much time for fun. Then, the official story goes, he had a Revelation, meeting Jesus Christ one afternoon in a cornfield. Jesus Christ told Martin Parsons to change his life immediately and prepare for the long struggle ahead. The struggle, of course, was against Satan and his earthly cohorts, of whom the communists were clearly the vanguard. At the time, Parsons said later, he didn't know a communist from a cow; this was before the Russian Revolution. But Jesus told him very clearly that Russia would try to conquer the world. Godless men would attempt to destroy all religion. The Thirteenth Tribe of Israel would return from its long exile and rouse the colored people of the earth and there would be many years of war, pillage, famine, rape, and miscegenation, not necessarily in that order. The dire warnings about miscegenation ended in the 1960's; the rest of the message remained essentially the same, from God's cornfield to our ears.

"I realized that Jesus was choosing me to lead us out of our wilderness," Parsons told *The American Weekly* in 1938. "I realized that I had a true mission. God had granted me certain gifts and now He told me to use them in His name."

Two months after the cornfield summit, Parsons transferred from the state agricultural college to a fundamentalist Bible school in South Carolina. He was graduated as a doctor of divinity, and returned to Iowa to preach the gospel. As a preacher, he avoided World War One, of course, but times remained lean in home front Iowa, even for a man with a direct mandate from God; the preaching competition was strong, the population sparse. But Parsons was soon gladdened by history: World War One was one confirmation of his Revelation, and the Russian Revolution another. The dread Bolsheviks provided the details he was to develop into a cosmic theory over the next half-century. Satan was alive and well, he said, and living in Moscow.

"Clearly the communists are the Thirteenth Tribe of Israel," he said, in a clip from the old *New York American*, dated May 1, 1929. "They have come to exact revenge, in the name of Satan. That is why the Thirteenth Tribe was cast out in the first place. This century will be the Lord's Great Test. We shall experience every sort of woe. But if we follow the leadership of Christ, we shall not simply endure, we shall conquer the forces of Satan for all eternity."

By 1924, Martin Parsons Senior had left Iowa for the fertile green valleys and golden shores of California. He was initially joined by thirteen followers; together they built a small church at the far end of the San Fernando Valley, which was then all farmland and orange groves. Two more historical events vaulted him from the role of ordinary small-time preacher into theological stardom. One was the Depression, which emptied the dust-blown farms of the Great Plains and drove Okies and Midwesterners over the Continental Divide into those green California valleys in search of salvation. The other event was radio.

"God allowed man to invent radio in order to combat Satan," Parsons Senior said in that *American Weekly* interview. "I am exercising God's will, sending the message of Jesus through God's own holy air."

Parsons Senior started small, at a marginal commercial station with a frail transmitter. But he had a gift for the medium. The articles all described his deep passionate voice, its quality of doom and accusation, its inordinate strength and conviction. In those early days, others spotted his talent for holding a radio audience. He soon moved to another station in Los Angeles, with a more powerful transmitter, and began to use his Sunday morning program to solicit funds for the building of a grand new church. It would be built in the desert emptiness of Orange County to the south. From the sun-blistered shacks of the Okie settlements, from the baffled exiles of Ohio and Nebraska and Ohio, the money began to flow, in quarters and dimes and dollar bills. And within a year, the First Church of Christ the Leader began to rise from the sands. Its most distinguishing architectural characteristics were a cross and a transmitter. Like all good Americans, Martin Parsons had realized a primary ambition: he had gone into business for himself.

Martin Junior was born in 1935, to the second of his father's three wives. Each of those women, as the Irish would say, were to die on the old man; in the photographs, they were interchangeably wan and pale women, who could have been sisters; they had long oval faces, as if Georgia O'Keefe had been painted by Grant Wood, except they had none of the character of either painter. The clips never said how Junior got along with his mother or father. They did say that he was brought up firmly in the rigid verities of the true faith and, as the only son, was groomed from the beginning to succeed his father. On weekends, Junior worked in the printing department of the ministry, helping produce the many pamphlets that cost about sixteen cents to print and were retailed for two bucks each at the end of the weekly broadcast. He printed transcripts of his father's broadcasts, too, which also went for two dollars a copy. He went to a good Baptist college and majored in communications, preparing well for the future transmission of the electronic gospel.

In the early black-and-white photographs that accompanied the articles, Junior was a handsome young man in a conventional California style. His dark hair was chopped into a crew cut that somehow managed to look stylish. His eyes were clear, undoubtedly blue, and in one picture, he was standing beside his father, wearing a short-sleeved sweater, a wide grin, chinos, white socks, and loafers. The letters on the sweater were CCL. His father seemed oddly embarrassed, like an immigrant standing beside a mysterious new son of America.

In the later pictures, Junior gradually changed. His hair grew fuller, thicker; the sideburns streaked with white. Chinos and loafers were gradually replaced by gray suits. Soon the hair was totally white, and he had come to resemble an anchor man from some TV station in the Midwest, the eyes steady as they peered at the cameras, the jawline firm, the hair a blown-dry masterpiece. I was certain, looking at the pictures, that he possessed the firmest handshake in any room he ever entered.

The later pictures were taken after that momentous announcement in 1957 that Junior was succeeding his father as the shepherd of their vast wired flock. Ordained by his father himself, Junior was a star within three years, and his vehicle was that most successful of organs of the Lord: television. At twenty-two, the young preacher moved into television as if he had been born in a studio; in a way, of course, he had. The message was essentially the same his father had peddled on radio, but the young man was slicker, more low-key, more intimate; in McLuhan's phrase, cooler. Looking at his face in the yellowing clips, I slowly remembered seeing him on TV somewhere in the South in the early 1960's, while lying on my back in a forgotten motel room, watching in admiration and astonishment. He had given up his father's rap about the Thirteenth Tribe, in deference, I suppose, to the FCC and the Anti-Defamation League. But the product was, in many ways, the mixture as before: anti-Communism, Americanism, Capitalism, and God.

Then, in 1967, there was a scandal. Suddenly, the son was off TV, the father brought back from retirement to replace him. There were now five hundred-odd stations to service; the show must go on. But the scandal was a murky one, barely covered by the New York papers; the Church of Christ the Leader didn't count many followers in the sinful precincts of New York. But part of the offstage drama almost certainly had been about sex.

"My son has sinned," the father said, in one of the news stories, "and sin must be punished."

When discussed in those grim and Calvinistic tones,

sin always meant sex. But there were no details and nothing more appeared in the New York papers about the Parsons family for almost two years. Then the *Bergen Evening Record* ran a story announcing that the Church of Christ the Leader had moved its national headquarters from California to New Jersey. The father said that he wanted to be closer to that capital of Satan, Sodom-by-the-Sea, New York City. They were talking now about having three hundred and seventy-five stations, and a few months later, as construction was finished on the new church complex in Fort Lee, there was an official announcement that Junior was coming back. God's network wasn't much different from the secular giants; when ratings go down, you bring on the old reliables.

"Jesus believes in redemption," Senior told a reporter who pressed him about Junior's past. "And so do I."

Marta had also brought me a thin folder of eight-by-ten glossies. Most of them were standard handout stuff. But one photograph gave me the connection I was looking for: it showed father and son at a banquet in Atlantic City in 1971. They were smiling for the photographers, and they were standing on either side of a man whose name and face meant more in Belfast than it ever would in Atlantic City. He had a thick fleshy face, a snarling defiant mouth, short cropped hair, and the head was crammed into the hard collar of a clergyman. I had seen him many times on television in Belfast, watched him rant in bleak medieval language from his pulpit in the Free Presbyterian Church; had even interviewed him once, long ago. His name was Ian Richard Kyle Paisley. As a young man, he had picked up a couple of mail order degrees in divinity from American correspondence schools, and welded them to his obvious gifts for inflamed rhetoric. More than any single man he was responsible for setting off the current round of violence in the North, and he did it with words. The words were full of ignorance and hatred, claiming knowledge of imaginary alliances between the Pope and the Soviets, proclaiming the eternal command of God Almighty that Ulster should remain forever British. Interviewing him that one time, I was prepared to accept him as another cynical theological politician, using fear and ignorance to secure a secular power base. I came away from the interview in a state of arctic chill. Paisley was worse than I had ever expected. He believed his brutal words.

And there he was, standing beside Martin Parsons, father and son.

I got out of bed, shaved and showered, my ribs still aching from Barney's kick, my swollen nose leaking slowly into my throat. But the adrenalin rush was strong now: there was a connection, fragile and circumstantial, between the Parsons people and the fanatical Protestant fundamentalists of Northern Ireland. I didn't think Ian Paisley would license murder, or order the bombing of an Irish bar in New York, or accept the killing of American politicians. But from the 1950's to the present, he had helped create men who could. Men who had, in fact, murdered Catholics, and would continue to murder Catholics in the name of God. Such men knew how to contact their friends in the United States. They would know how to find their way to the Church of Christ the Leader. So did I.

I was drying myself when the phone rang. I picked it off the wall in the bathroom.

"How's the old *nariz*, big boy?" Marta said.

"Bigger," I said. "And hey, thanks for that stuff from the *News*. It helps. It helps a lot."

"Do me a favor," she said. "Don't explain it to me. The Bronx is hard enough to understand without having to figure out the Irish or the Jesus nuts."

"I won't even try," I said.

"And you better call your service," she said. "I called over there to see if some bimbo answered. Someone you stashed there while you passed out in my bed. I got the service, lucky for you. They said you should call right away. A couple of messages are urgent."

When she hung up, I called the service. Charlie Kelly had called twice. Jimmy Breslin had called from the *News* and left a one-word message about my Irish piece: "Okay." And there were six other messages. Five were from Elaine in Spain. She had called from two separate numbers. The other was from Sheila Rafferty. She left a number.

"She said it was very important," the woman from the service said. "Very, very important."

I dialed Sheila's number. A man picked up.

"Briscoe?"

"Yes."

"Give me your number and then hang up," the voice said. There was no accent to the voice, no edge, no burr. "Someone will call you back within a minute."

I gave him the number, hung up, and waited. My stomach tightened. Fear, deep and formless, made its move. The phone rang.

"Briscoe?" the familiar voice said. It was Sheila.

"Yeah."

"You're going to go away for a few weeks," she said. "You're going to forget everything you know. You're going to forget who you saw in Belfast, and you're going to forget me."

"I am?"

"Yes, you are."

"Why?" I said.

"Hold on, and you'll know why," she said. "Someone wants to talk to you."

She put the phone down hard on a table, and went away somewhere. I could hear a door open and close. Then footsteps coming back. Then the phone being picked up.

"Daddy?" my daughter April said. "Daddy, I'm sorry. I—"

Click. The dial tone went through my skull like a drill.

21 I called Charlie Kelly and told him that April had been kidnapped. I told him about Sheila Rafferty and what I knew about her. I told him that she was connected to the IRA. But I didn't tell him everything. I didn't want some crew-cutted assholes from the FBI shooting their way to April. I didn't want fanatics using my daughter as a shield. I was going to have to do some of this work myself. Charlie took notes, quickly and professionally. He said he would get to the FBI right away, and he told me to let him know where I was going to be, in case the Feds wanted to talk to me. He didn't mention a biology teacher for his daughter.

Then I called Elaine in Torremolinos. She wasn't at either of the two numbers she had left on my service. They must have been police stations. I called her at home. The boyfriend answered. He told me that Elaine was exhausted and couldn't be disturbed. I told him to get her on the phone or I'd have him burned to death. He told me to wait *un momento*. As I waited, my stomach churned again. I had to move. I had to do something. I had to go and find these people and get my daughter back or I'd get sick and die. I knew it; I would die. Cancer would come up out of my stomach and kill me. It would eat me. It would eat me from the inside out. Cancer of foolishness, carelessness, romantic stupidity; cancer of the man who always had to follow the action. The boyfriend finally came back.

"*Un momentito*," he said.

Then Elaine was there, her voice slurred, sobbing. She told me about the men who had come to the house the day before, in broad daylight, wearing ski masks, holding guns. Two of them. Two men. No accents. No, they didn't have accents. Oh, maybe they did; Elaine wasn't sure. The chauffeur had the day off. The cook was on vacation. The two men hadn't said much. She had been gagged and tied up and shoved into a closet. Oh, no, that was later. First, April

114

tried to hit one of the men, and the man had slapped her hard with the back of his hand and knocked her down. When Elaine protested, he punched her and she fell under the kitchen table. Then he kicked her. After that, they tied her up. Maybe they did have accents. She was in the closet a long time. Eight hours. Nine hours. It was hard to say. Finally Alex came home. The boyfriend. He was drunk. He'd been out somewhere. She didn't know where. He found Elaine. She had heard him come in and kicked at the closet door until he heard her. Then she had called the Spanish police. And she had tried to find the American consul. She was in the police station all night. She had tried to find me. She had tried me all night. She had gone from one police station to another. Yes, she had asked the Spanish police to keep the story out of the newspapers. On a kidnapping, they said they would obey her wishes. That was what they said. Then she had come home. She had taken too much valium. She was sure April was dead.

"Listen, Elaine," I said. "She's alive. I talked to her on the phone fifteen minutes ago."

"Alive?" she said through the Valium blur. "Where?"

"Here," I said. "In New York."

I told her a little about what I knew, but not everything; in some odd way, I still was afraid of her wrath. I knew and she knew that our daughter was in terrible trouble because of me. There was no way I could avoid that. But I didn't want her feeling more helpless or more furious on the other side of the ocean. I told her that the cops and the FBI were working on the case and everything possible was being done. But she didn't accept that. She was coming to New York on the next plane. Her voice hardened, shaking off the foggy edge of the Valium.

"Goddamn you, Sam," she said.

"Please don't say anything else," I said. "It's bad enough."

"You and your twisted little life," she said. "I hope you're proud of yourself. The big newspaperman."

"Shut up," I said.

There was a pause. Then: "What are you going to do?"

"Get her back," I said, and hung up.

22 In the old days, Fort Lee was a mob town. The hoodlums made their money in New York and kept their girlfriends in the city's towers. But they lived with their families across the river, at the New Jersey end of the George Washington Bridge. Their homes were local tourist attractions, with wire fences and floodlit lawns, statues of Our Lady of Fatima beside the doors, and their wives and children locked away within. Driving over the bridge in Marta's blue Ford, on this brilliant spring morning, I tried to shove off the terrible present by drifting into the past. I remembered going to Fort Lee once as a kid reporter when a hoodlum named Tony Bender disappeared. His wife let me in, and we sat in the kitchen as she told me what a good man Tony was, and how he would go out of his way to buy in stores that gave Green Stamps. She reached up into a closet and took down a large Green Stamps book and laid it on the kitchen table, under the watchful eye of the bleeding Jesus framed over the door. "Tony was such a good man," she said, "that he would sit here with the Green Stamps. And he would lick, and I would put." Nobody had seen Tony Bender for eight days at that point, and nobody would ever see him again, but his wife was the supreme realist: she talked about him only in the past tense. That was a simpler time, in so many ways; the mob guys worked only for money and themselves; they would have thought it insane for anyone to risk death or jail over abstractions. They would not die for their country, they would not fight armed British soldiers. They would not go on hunger strikes. They weren't nationalists or patriots. They were just hoodlums. But as hoodlums, they would never have done what Sheila Rafferty and her people had done to my daughter. If they

116

wanted me, they'd have come after me themselves. They never went after children. They never touched family.

But most of the old hoodlums were gone now, some shot in the ear, some dead of cancer, others camped in dusty retirement in the condominiums north of Miami, close to the racetrack. I wished I could call one of them and ask for a favor. I needed a gun. I had a gun back in the loft. But if I went to get it I might never make it to the elevator. I had to do what I was doing without a gun, and hope for the best. Charlie Kelly would go to that phone booth and dust it for prints. He and the Feds would be all over the Irish bars in search of Sheila Rafferty. But I could deal with these people in ways that the police couldn't. I didn't need a search warrant. I didn't need to read anyone his Miranda rights. I could come across this river, into Fort Lee, and try to make a connection that would lead to my daughter, or have it end up as a dry well, and I could do it my own way. I didn't think the IRA would do what was done to April. I didn't think Steel could order that. I didn't think that after what happened to my uncle Frank the IRA would go after me. No. Someone else was after me. And Sheila Rafferty was working for those people. She might have been duped by them, thinking she was taking orders from Steel when she was actually being directed by others. Or. Maybe. If. Maybe. My head was too full of maybes. The road became crowded with images: Uncle Frank, that wild ride in the night of Switzerland, the destruction of McDaid's, poor Barney Mullins and that wrecked kid Sandy, and the image of my daughter trying to strike a masked man and being knocked down. Images like billboards on the road to Fort Lee.

Most of the gangsters were gone, but Fort Lee looked prosperous. New apartment houses grew everywhere, muscling each other for better views of the skyline across the Hudson. The streets were clean. The trees were beginning to stir, eager for spring. I drifted down Elm Avenue for a few blocks and then, ahead, saw a white concrete wall, and beyond the wall, the Church of Christ the Leader. I knew it by the cross and the transmitter.

I parked the blue Ford a block away, on a street of older houses with porches and lawns and shrubs. It was the kind of place to which people once moved for the sake of the kids, and probably still did, except that there were no kids anywhere in sight. The kids were in school, or riding around listening to Bruce Springsteen, full of beer and anger. The local kids were probably getting ready for New York, where they could go next day, and wear funny green hats for St. Patrick's Day, and throw up in doorways, and then drive home drunk through the tunnels, and die in crashes on the turnpike. These kids really didn't care what their parents did for them. They didn't want niceness, and grass, and shrubs, and porches, and in a way, I didn't blame them. They could die in the midst of their little rebellions, but I envied all of them at that moment. Their lives might be empty, pointless, even despairing; but they were not, like April, in the hands of fanatics.

I walked up the street, chilled by the wind off the river. There was a main gate, with the name of the church handsomely lettered in three-dimensional Caslon. A gravel drive went up to a low flat concrete-block building that was painted white and looked carved from salt in the bright cold sunshine. About two hundred people were lined up patiently on the gravel drive outside the building. A special cop, lean and fit in a gray uniform, sat inside a windowed gatehouse.

"Hi," I said, giving him a good shit-kicker smile. He gave me the same smile back.

"Here for the tapin', brother?"

"Sure am."

"Just mosey on up there and wait on the line. They're finishin' one now, and the next one should start in, oh, half an hour."

"Thanks, brother," I said, and walked up the gravel driveway to the end of the line. A middle-aged couple stood in front of me. The man was a paunchy fifty, his rain hat and cheap, black, horn-rimmed glasses making him look like Billy Carter. His wife had a dusty pallor, and thick chins, and was wearing a tan carcoat lined with down. She was chewing gum.

"Oh, I hope we get in," she said.

"Don't worry, dear, we'll get in."

"I hope so. 'Member that time we came all the way here and couldn't get in?"

"That was Easter, dear. They had all the members from the rest of the country here. This is different. Easter won't be for awhile yet."

"When d'you think we'll be on TV?" she said. "I mean, so we can see ourselves?"

"Soon, I guess. Two or three weeks, I reckon."

"Oh, the kids'll be so happy."

Long ago, they must have lived in the South; the speech rhythms were southern, although long residence in the North had removed the softness of the drawl. I looked off to the right, where three private houses stood on a slight hill. They were painted white. Their porches evoked the lost America of *The Saturday Evening Post* and Norman Rockwell, but there was something chilly and remote about them, too, as if they'd actually been painted by Charles Sheeler. No human faces appeared in the windows or on those white porches with their silent swings. One of the white houses was larger than the others. To the left of the houses, a path led over the hill to a solid two-story brick building. It looked like the administrative center of a small college. Behind the building was a parking lot, with four Cadillacs, several pickup trucks, a couple of vans, and a dump truck lined up against a chain link fence. At the top of the fence, separating the compound from the rest of the world, I could see barbed wire.

"It's almost time," the woman said, looking anxiously at her watch. "They should be finished."

They were. The doors of the large church opened, and the flock poured out. They looked like clones of the people who were waiting on line to get in, dressed in the checkered wool coats, hunting jackets, windbreakers and zippered carcoats of the suburban working class. The adults were middle-aged, and a few had brought along children, as freshly scrubbed as Sunday morning. I had never taken April to a place like this; the two of us had gone to zoos and concert halls, to museums and Yankee Stadium and Coney Island. Once I'd taken her with me to the Concord Hotel in the Catskills to see Muhammad Ali train; Elaine had protested bitterly about violence and *machismo*, while April squealed in delight and was charmed by Ali, the master charmer. I looked at these scrubbed kids, waiting on line, knowing that the cops and the Feds were already working on the kidnapping, hoping that I got there first. I also hoped, before the cops arrived, that I could hurt someone. My head began to swarm with anxiety and violence, and then I stopped myself, afraid that the people around me could read my true story on my face. I focused on them again. They looked like extras in a movie set in the early fifties, some quiet year before dope and rock 'n' roll and gay rights, any year before Dallas or Vietnam or men who walked on the moon.

They looked like nice people, most of them, searching for some kind of certainty among the confusions of the world. I thought I understood that part of them. I often wished for certainty myself. But I could never accept the surrender that certainty demanded, the surrender of intelligence, choice, sensuality, and what used to be called a sense of humanity. For a long time I had understood the old values were all that mattered; but I also knew that civilization was terribly fragile. So fragile that I would gladly use a gun to get my daughter.

Our line moved quickly to the entrance, and we left the vibrating brilliance of the sunshine for the sudden darkness of the vestibule. Two dark-suited young men were at the door, their hair cut short, handing out envelopes with seat numbers hand-lettered on the outside. One of them looked up at me, momentarily dubious, and then handed me an envelope without saying a word. I followed the couple along the length of the vestibule, and then turned left into the church.

The Church of Christ the Leader opened before us, flooded with the hard white of TV lights. The walls were austere, and the ceiling soared away in some trick perspective that made it seem higher than Notre-Dame. Music played insistently, the music of militant Protestantism.

I went up the aisle on my right, following the others, partially blinded by the lights. I sat on the end of a pew and opened the envelope. Inside were a handful of leaflets and a pledge card. Obviously it would not look right to take up a collection while being taped for TV.   .

Then, with everyone seated, and the doors closed behind us, the room hushed. The bright TV lights turned away from the audience and then went off completely. Suddenly the altar was plunged into darkness and the side aisles seemed to vanish. A disembodied voice boomed from a sound system.

"Welcome to the Church of Christ the Leader," the voice said. "We are joined here today to worship the true God, leader of all mankind, creator of the universe. All of us are equal in his eyes, all of us are his creations. All of us worship at his feet. All of us shall join him in eternity, or be cast by him into the endless torments of hell. . . ."

The voice boomed on, the words a fearful monotone; my eyes slowly adjusted to the scene on the altar. There were at least three cameras, presided over by crew members in formal gray suits. A fourth camera was bolted to the pulpit on the left, aimed at the audience. A railing separated the audience from the altar, and at the foot of the rail another dozen young men in gray suits stood six feet apart, their hands together in front of them, like off-duty prizefighters waiting to be introduced at a big fight.

Abruptly, the voice finished: ". . . . and the word was God!" There was a sudden brilliant explosion of light, triumphant chords of music, and Martin Parsons Senior was alone on the altar in a black cassock. It was difficult to hear his voice now because he was speaking softly and intimately for the cameras, without amplification. There were TV monitors on the aisles, and the attentive eyes of the flock immediately switched from the real person before them on the altar to his televised image. I'd seen people do that before, while watching the "Johnny Carson Show" in the studio in Burbank.

The old man had kept most of his hair, gray and combed straight back, but his face had the lost bitter look of an aging general. Makeup added a layer of ashen tan, and brackets cut into his face from the side of his nose to his chin, giving him a look of permanent disappointment. He spoke for about five minutes, his brow corrugating with emphasis, italicizing his main points. Then he was finished, and the light shifted to the pulpit, without missing a beat, and Junior began to speak.

The moment was theatrically masterful, and Junior rose to it. His words were more distinct than his father's, his presence more defined. The old man walked to his side of the altar and sat down heavily and sadly and never again looked at his son. The son spoke firmly to the crowd before him, and to all the people who would see him on their TV sets.

". . . The world is starved for leadership. We see it on the local level, where it becomes increasingly difficult to get even a simple pothole filled, while hundreds of layabouts live off the public dole. We see it on the national level, where inflation is rampant, where the national will is sapped by pornography and excess. We see it on the international level, where the communist tide rolls through Asia and Africa and Afghanistan, unchecked and unre-marked. . . ."

Junior wore a look of detached, sour amusement while he spoke, and never consulted notes. He looked older than his photographs. The hair was completely white, worn like a crown above the deeply-tanned face, with its neat precise nose lost in flesh that was beginning finally to sag. On the monitors, his eyes were a clear, impassive marble blue, and once his right hand brushed the sides of his hair almost reverently. But it was his voice that was his great weapon, and obviously the most valuable inheritance from his father. The voice had range and timbre, baritone lows, a dramatic middle range, the threat of true power if he chose to reach for the gallery. An actor's voice. And not just a stage actor.

An actor made for television. An actor who could do the small things. Who could make you trust him. Junior could enter your living room via the tube, turn on those baby blues and make you believe almost anything.

". . . The only leadership is in Christ. The only hope is in Christ. The only joy is in Christ. The only relief from suffering is from Christ. The—"

Someone tapped my shoulder. I looked up. It was Manning.

23 I stood up, and shoved him into the side aisle. He skittered backwards, surprised and rubber-legged; I started moving through the pew away from him. The nice men and women looked suddenly angry as I bumped them, their concentration on the monitors broken, but Junior never broke the roll of his rhetoric. The words of damnation and redemption poured out for the benefit of the unspooling videotape, and when I glanced at Junior, I saw two figures move away from the altar rail. When I reached the center aisle, they were waiting for me.

"You can leave quietly," said the short blond one, "or you can make trouble."

"Quietly," I said. "Why not?"

They stood on either side of me, like soldiers escorting a cashiered officer to the firing squad. We walked down the center aisle to the rear of the church. The doughy faces in the pews turned momentarily to look at us, their eyes baffled, as if trying to decide if I was part of the show. Maybe I was an agent of the Thirteenth Tribe. Maybe I had showed up drunk. Maybe I was a plainclothes communist. Whatever the reason, I was being escorted out of the building by two soldiers of the Lord.

They slammed me roughly through the double doors into the darkness of the vestibule. Manning was waiting. His eyes glittered. He threw a right hand at me, but I'd expected that, and bent under the punch, ripped a hook to his belly, whipped around, sliced with my elbow at the short blonde, hit bone, rammed the third one backward with my head and kept going through the front doors.

The sun was blinding. I ran through the glare down the path, gravel crunching under my feet, toward the gate. I heard doors open behind me, and muffled shouts in the still air. The guard stepped out of the little guardhouse, gun in hand.

He raised the gun, as if the gesture alone would stop me. But I kept coming, spreading my arms, showing my empty hands, and smiling at him. The smile apparently disarmed him. He lowered the gun. And then I banged into him with a body block, knocking him over, reached down, scooped up the gun, and kept running. Outside the gate, I stopped at a giant elm, turned, saw Manning and the two others, coming on a run. I raised the gun. The blonde dived for the ground. I fired twice, over their heads. The noise was enormous in the still morning. Manning and the other one stopped. I fired one more shot and they fell to the ground, too. I ran out of their view around a corner to the car, shoving the .45 in my belt. Then I drove quickly and carefully through the side streets, until I found a small shopping center. I pulled in and parked.

All right, I thought: now you have a gun, what are you going to do with it?

I locked the car, and went into a coffee shop. I sat down at the counter and ordered an English muffin and a cup of tea. I also bought the *Times*. There was nothing in the paper about any of this: nothing about the kidnapping of my daughter; nothing about the explosion that had killed McDaid; nothing about Ireland. There were at least two versions of reality, and I was now living in the unreported one. I went to a wall phone and called Marta Torres at her office. I told her what had happened—that I'd had to give the kidnappers her phone number, and that it was possible they could track the number to an address. I told her to rent a suite at the Mayflower Hotel on Central Park West and charge it to my account.

"Why don't you let the Feds handle this?" she said, in an exasperated way.

"They'll do their part of it," I said. "I'll do mine."

"*Macho* bullshit."

"Yes," I said, and hung up.

I paid the check and tucked the *Times* under my arm. Then I went back to the car and drove toward the Church of Christ the Leader. I avoided the main gate and cruised around the edges of the compound. The buildings were behind a chain fence about ten feet high. It was wired at the top, but I didn't know whether the wire was electrified. The grounds were deserted. At the opposite end of the compound from the church, I saw another gate, and beyond the gate in a parking lot, men were moving quickly. One of them was Manning. I turned into a side street, kept going out of sight, then doubled back and parked on a rise, with a clear view of the lot.

A crew cut young man in a gray suit opened the gates, and the first two cars came out. They headed straight up the street on which I was parked. I squashed deep into the seat, with the *Times* over me and the gun in my hand. The first two cars were packed with men in gray suits. Then one of the Fleetwood Cadillacs went by, a deep bronze job glistening in the sun. One of the vans followed. They were moving fast.

I lay still for another five minutes, but there were no more cars. The street was quiet again. I sat up. The crew cut young man sat inside the gate on a chair, reading a book.

Folding the *Times* to the classified section, I got out of the car. I walked down the block, glancing at the *Times*, and then at addresses on the houses. A dog barked loudly. The young guard looked up from his book. I stared at the *Times*, and tried to act puzzled. I retraced my steps, deliberately looking from address to newspaper. Then I shook my head, trying to appear lost and confused. I walked briskly and innocently across the street to the gate. There was a heavy padlock and chain holding the gates together.

"Hey, I'm trying to find 271 Elm Street," I said. "I can't figure it out."

The young man stood up. He was only a kid. Eighteen, maybe. Or younger. He had been reading the Bible, of course. I tapped my copy of the *Times*.

"The ad says there's a two-bedroom apartment at 271 Elm Street," I said, "but I can't find that address."

He pressed against the fence, peering at the ad in the *Times*. I shoved the gun through the chain links into his belly.

"Open the gate, boy," I said, "or I'll put a hole in your fucking belly so big you could park a bus in it."

The color drained from his face. He froze.

"Nice and easy, now," I said. "Don't shout. Don't try to be brave. Just open the gate. Nice and easy."

"Who are you?" he whispered hoarsely.

"The wrath of God," I said.

I could hear recorded religious music playing in the distance. The boy reached into the pocket of the gray suit for a ring of keys. He opened the padlock. I slipped inside, and took the lock and put it in my pocket.

"Where do I find Mister Parsons?" I said. We were standing together inside the fence like two men discussing baseball. I slipped the *Times* over the gun, and stood sideways, with the muzzle pointed at his belly.

"Which one, sir?" he said. His short-cropped hair bristled like a cat in danger.

"Both."

"Reverend Parsons Junior, he went out," the kid said. "He just left in his Caddy, sir. His father's up in his house, I guess." His face trembled. "He usually takes a nap after services. He's old, you know."

"I know," I said. I could see the largest white house beyond a cluster of low concrete buildings. "Is that the house?"

"Yes, sir."

"Well, I'll tell you what," I said. "I don't think I'll kill you. I think you'll walk along with me up to that house. I think you'll be taking me to my appointment. You'll act very normal. You'll wave to people. You'll smile. You'll act as if there was nothing wrong."

"Yes, sir."

"You won't try to do anything stupid."

"Yes, sir."

"I don't want to hurt you. I don't want to hurt the old man. I just have to talk to him about something."

"I understand."

"Let's go."

We left the parking lot along another gravel path that took us past the low white buildings. The area was completely deserted. Through the windows I could see the machinery of the God business—offset presses, computers for typesetting, accounting and mailing lists, stacks of books and mailing envelopes. Because it was taping day in the electronic ministry, the workers must have been given the day off; one wouldn't want the faithful to get the wrong idea. We stopped in the shade of one of the office buildings. I tried the door. It was open. I stepped inside and motioned to the young man.

"Come here," I said.

He stepped inside and I slugged him with the butt of the gun. He fell hard and I dragged him behind a row of mimeograph machines. On a table there were stacks of pamphlets carrying the headline: "Beware the Earth Day Fraud!" A subhead asked: "Why is Earth Day on Lenin's Birthday?" I crumpled one and shoved it in the kid's mouth. Then I tore a phone out of the wall, snapped off the cord, and tied the kid's hands to his feet, thinking: I'm almost as good at this as Barney Mullins. I left the kid lying behind the mimeograph machine.

From the window of the office building I stared at the big house. It was a strange mixture of architectural styles: a porch out of the Gilded Age; cupolas and stained glass windows in the upper stories, sliding glass doors from California on the first floor, wicker chairs and plastic tables on the lawn. There was absolutely no human activity inside or out. The music was much louder now, blasting hymns from a speaker lodged in a tree. If the Parsons people had grabbed my daughter, they would have been fools to bring her here. But standing there, drowned by the music, I knew that anything was possible. These were people who believed.

I stepped outside, and, holding the gun in my jacket pocket, I hurried across the space between the buildings to the big house. I thought: this is too easy.

It was.

I tried the front door.

It jerked open. The little blond man was standing there with a gun in his hand. The gun was made larger by a silencer.

He seemed as surprised as I was. I chopped at his gun arm, and he made a pained sound, but held on to the gun. I kicked at him, driving him inside, and went in after him, slamming the door behind me. He whirled and fired. The silencer smothered the sound. It was as if he had fired a dart at me. I went down, rolling, and whirled. He fired twice more, splintering the woodwork behind me. I groaned.

He paused, stood up, and stared at me.

I shot him between the eyes.

24 It was a moment in a hunt. His hunt. And my hunt. I was tracking other prey, but found this young blond hunter trying to kill me. I had killed him instead. I wish I could say I felt sick. I wish I had felt something in that moment. I didn't. I was still caught up in my own hunt. And so I turned to the stairs, the house awash in the music of the risen Christ. The old man must be up there. I went to the front door, locked it, stared out at the deserted grounds. There were no people anywhere in sight.

I climbed the stairs briskly, crouched over to make a smaller target. There were no pictures anywhere, and no flowers. The walls were painted in various tones of gray, and there were no splashes of color in drapes or curtains. There had never been women here; I was certain of that; the house was a giant monument to denial. I turned at the landing. At the far end of the landing was an open door, leading to a bright room. I could see a desk, but nothing else. I walked quietly to the door, and then jumped into the room gripping the gun in both hands.

And felt immediately foolish.

Martin Parsons lay on a brown leather couch. The fingers of his hands made a small steeple on his chest. He stared at me.

"So you've come at last," he said.

"I want to talk to you."

"You don't have to talk," he said. "Just do it. I've been waiting for that bullet for fifty years."

He was very still.

"I'm not here to kill you," I said. "I'm here to find my daughter."

"Your daughter?"

"She's been kidnapped," I said. "From her home in Spain. Somebody here might know where she is. You, for instance."

"Spain?" he said. "Kidnapped?"

I repeated myself. He looked at me with incomprehension in his eyes.

"I'll call Franco," he said. "He's a personal friend. He'll get to the bottom of this."

"Franco's dead," I said. "And the Spanish police are working on it."

"Franco's not dead," he said. "I saw him yesterday."

"Yeah?"

"Now there's a man who understands the world and God's mission," he said. He rose from the couch, and tottered toward an easy chair beside the window. Through the panes, I could see an expanse of lawn, the church white against the budding carpet of spring. "I didn't accept his religion. He was a Catholic, after all. But he knew the dangers of the Thirteenth Tribe. He understood the seventeen-year cycles, too; the sun, the moon, the earth in tandem, and what it meant to history. He knew that the Lord wanted order. He understood the wedding of the bride of death."

The man was insane.

I had expected a charlatan, a hustler. I found a lunatic. A lunatic, or a goddamned good actor.

"Where is Manning?" I said.

"Manning? That fellow who works for my son?"

"Lean, stupid."

"Yes. Yes, I've met that young man. A good soldier. Yes." He paused. "Well, in the planets, there *are* waves, you know. They exert enormous pressure on the tides of men. Roosevelt was their victim. He hired Morgenthau, and the circle closed. I explained that to the Princess Anastasia when she arrived here from Hong Kong. The Morris Plan didn't help, either. It led only to missiles and the single tax. I've tried to explain that to my son. But he is Satan's child. He has lain down with the whore of Babylon, with the mother of abominations. Only the Roman Empire ever united Europe. That was why the Lord granted me the master key. Roosevelt wanted to make Satanism the state religion. And my son, he slept with water mocassins. We had to burn the devil from his flesh. Would you like some tea?"

"No, thank you," I said.

"What was it you came to see me for, if not to deliver me to the Lord?"

"A young girl."

"Ah, yes. Your daughter."

"You haven't seen her?"

"No. But once I saw a mountain dance in the twilight. It rose off the floor of the desert and turned in the light. The Lord was there to ease my doubt, to shore up my weakness." A pause. "Pearl Harbor was predicted. The atomic bomb was predicted. The Lord knows, and His ways are mysterious, but He knows. He knows."

"What do you think about Northern Ireland?"

He turned and something hard entered his eyes. "The anti-Christ is everywhere now. Triumph is inevitable. The sand blows through wicked streams."

"Do you know Ian Paisley?"

"No. Is he a Christian?"

"Sort of."

He brooded. I glanced at the door. There was a large metal key in the lock. The old man repeated Paisley's name.

"I remember him," he said after awhile. "Large fellow. A white man. Big voice. Great preacher. Yes. Yes, I remember."

"Would you work with him?"

"Work with him?" he said loudly. "We sent him money. My son brought it to him personally. Yes. His name was. His name. His name was Ian. His. Name was."

He sat back, his face exhausted. He put his hands flat on the desk.

"There are so few miracles and the universe is vast," he said. "We have seed to plant. Harvests to gather. If Franco had conquered Roosevelt, the New Deal would never have polluted the country and Romanism would not now be rife. I told Franco that. We were quail hunting in the Pyrenees. The crab apple trees touched the clouds. We saw lizards on the face of the moon. But the women never saw them. . . ."

He was very still now. And then I realized that he was sleeping.

I searched the house, opening all the doors to rooms and closets, checking the attic and the cellar. There was no sign that April had ever been there. I went out without looking back at the small blond hunter who was now with Jesus.

25 I came down off the George Washington Bridge into Harlem and drove straight to Small's Paradise. In Harlem, if nowhere else, I'd be safe. Jimmy Burnett looked up from his drink when I walked in. His smooth brown face creased as he focused on my nose.

"Jesus Christ," he said. "You look like Basilio after Robinson got through with him."

"You should've seen me last night."

"Get this man a drink," he said. "Irish, rocks." He

turned back to me as the bartender reached for the Dewar's. "What do you need, my man?"

"More help," I said. "Heavy help this time."

He left his stool and walked to the jukebox and played "Brown Sugar" by the Rolling Stones. You can't get much louder than that. When he came back to the bar, I told him that April had been kidnapped, and that the Feds and the local bacon were working on it. I told him that it might be connected to something Walker Smith was working on. I didn't want Walker Smith to get hurt. I particularly didn't want Jimmy Burnett to get hurt, for introducing me to Walker Smith. But most of all, I wanted my daughter back alive, and that's where the heavy help came in.

"Man," Jimmy Burnett said, "if you could major in trouble, you'd have a Ph.D."

"With honors."

"Well, look, man. Walker can't come here, for obvious reasons. And things bein' the way they are, you can't go there."

"Yeah."

The bartender stood discreetly on the far end of the oval bar, reading a paper, out of earshot.

"So tell me what kind of help you need, man," he said. "I'll pass it on."

"I need to find some people before the Feds do," I said. "A woman named Sheila Rafferty, worked in a place named McDaid's in Queens until it was blown up two nights ago. An ex-fighter named Barney Mullins." He took out a small pad and a fat Mont Blanc fountain pen and began making notes. I told him as much as I knew about Sheila and Barney, and he took the notes in silence. Sonny Rollins was now playing "Easy Living" on the juke. "And I want to find a guy named Martin Parsons. He should be in one of the midtown hotels, but you never know." I described Junior for him, too. "If he's spotted, call this guy." I gave him Charlie Kelly's numbers.

"You sound like you wanna hire a nigger police department," Jimmy said.

"Somethin' like that," I said. The whiskey tasted rich

and strong. "And there's the most important thing. Important for Walker Smith and important for me. If he decides he's gonna go through with that transaction—he'll know what I mean—tell him to hold it up until I know my daughter's safe. There's no reason why he should. Money is money, a business deal is a business deal. Tell him I won't try to stop the deal. I won't call the cops or the Feds, no matter what he decides. But if he can hold it up until I'm sure, I'd appreciate it. Tell him I'll call you here and you can let him know."

"Anything else?"

"Yeah," I said. "I have to get rid of a gun. And I need another one."

"You don't need Walker Smith for that, man."

"I killed a guy with it, Jimmy."

"That's why they make them, Sam. That's what they're for."

He put the notebook in his pocket and went out to the street. I had another Scotch. Paul Desmond's great record of "Take Four" began to play, and I flashed on nights at various tables, sitting up until closing time with Paul; New York was an emptier place since he died. I got a dollar's worth of dimes from the bartender and went to the pay phone. I gave an overseas operator my credit card number and a number in Belfast. I held on.

After awhile, an Irish baritone answered: "Sinn Fein Information Bureau."

"My name is Sam Briscoe," I said crisply. "A few days ago in Belfast, I interviewed a very important member of the Republican movement. You should know about it. That same week, my uncle Frank was murdered. Do you know what I'm talking about?"

"Aye."

"Well, something terrible has happened which you should know about," I said. "Here is my number in New York." I gave him the number of the pay phone. "Call me back from a safe phone, and I'll explain."

"Righto," the voice said, and hung up.

I dropped another dime in the slot, dialed 555-1212, and asked the operator for a number in Queens. Jack McDaid, I said. Or John McDaid. She found a number under "J. McDaid." I thanked her and then dialed the number. Mary McDaid answered. I told her who I was.

"Oh, yes," she said. "I've read your articles. Very good."

"Mary, has the FBI been around to see you?"

"No, not recently," she said. "Why should they?"

"It's very complicated, Mary, and hard to explain over the phone. But I have to know everything you can tell me about Sheila Rafferty."

"That whore."

"I understand how you feel, Mary. But this really is a matter of life and death. Your husband is dead. There could be a lot more people dead, and one of them is my daughter."

I told her about April, but nothing else.

"What does that whore have to do with it?"

"She might be a turncoat," I said. "I think she's working for the other side."

The operator demanded five cents for the next five minutes, please. I fed three dimes into the slot to keep her quiet. And when the operator's recorded voice was gone, Mary McDaid began to talk. It obviously wasn't easy for her. She talked about how McDaid, at first, told her about this new woman who worked at the bar, a narrow back, but a real Republican. Then he stopped talking about her, and Mary McDaid knew that something had happened; his silence was like a confession.

"Jack McDaid was always a silent man," she said bitterly. "Because he had lived his life with everything to hide. Him and his bloody underground organization. Him and his bloody IRA."

She lived with her suspicions in her own kind of silence. She had the children to raise, the house to run. But then Jack went too far: he began to stay out all night. His excuse was always the same—IRA business. He always told her first, so that she wouldn't worry. And always it was

IRA: meetings, deals, plans. She didn't believe him. And disbelief ate into her like an ulcer. One night he called to say he wouldn't be home until late in the morning, and Mary said, okay, fine, all right, and she carried her disbelief into the car, and drove out to Queens before closing time, and waited in the shadows of the El.

"He left with his whore," she told me. "They were the last to leave, and that was worse. It meant everybody in the bar knew what they were. These were people I'd see from time to time, when I came to some party or get-together. They knew. And they had to talk to me, and laugh with me, and act as if nothing was going on. Well, they went to Jack's car. I had to know as much as was knowable. So I followed them. Somehow I felt happy. It was as if knowing was enough. Knowing told me I wasn't some silly woman. That I had guessed right. I followed them all the way to Brooklyn."

"To Brooklyn?"

"Aye. They went to a house near Prospect Park. A brownstone. On Carroll Street, I believe."

Bingo.

"Do you have the address?"

"I believe I do," she said. "I wrote it down somewhere. Hold on, just a wee minute."

Jimmy Burnett came hurrying in the door, and looked alarmed when he saw me talking on the pay phone. I opened the door to the booth to talk to him, and then Mary McDaid came back on the phone.

"It was 432 Carroll Street," she said. "Their own little love nest. Later I had someone check the ownership for me, down at the Hall of Records, you know? And Jack owned it. He'd never told me a word about it, but he owned it, it was in his name. There we were, out in Queens, strugglin' to make ends meet, and he had his lovely little nest in Brooklyn, and his whore. Just thinkin' of it makes the blood boil. Jack McDaid. The son of a bitch. God forgive me."

Jimmy was signaling me not to talk anymore, making a cutting sign at his throat.

"Well, thank you, Mrs. McDaid," I said. "You've really been a giant help."

"God bless," she said, and hung up.

Jimmy was standing there over me. "Jesus, man," he said. "The fuckin' DEA is sure to have the motherfucker bugged."

"I never mentioned drugs," I said. "I talked about men and women. How'd you make out?"

"He'll do what he can about the people," Jimmy said. "He'll get his people lookin'. But he said business was business. He said you'd understand."

I laughed; I understood, all right. He was talking about more than a million dollars. He would take payment, make delivery and get his people out of there. Everything else was sentimentality.

"What about the piece?"

"Let's take a little ride around the block."

We started for the door when the phone rang. The bartender sighed and went to answer it. He nodded at me. The Irish baritone was on the line.

"What can I do for ye, Mister Briscoe?"

I told him what had happened to my daughter, and that I thought the IRA were going to blow up the Plaza Hotel, an event which could be the stupidest piece of politics in IRA history.

"Blow up the Plaza Hotel?" he said. "Not us, Mister. We're not that bloody stupid."

"I've got to get a message to Steel."

"I can't do that for you."

"Why?"

"Steel is in New York."

"To run this operation?"

"I've already said too much," he said, and hung up.

We drove down Adam Clayton Powell Boulevard in Jimmy's black Oldsmobile. He was the only man I'd ever met who played Charlie Parker with strings on his tape deck, and he played the music very loud. The streets were full of women shopping, junkies nodding, businessmen hurrying in and out of banks. Jimmy drove as if he were going to a specific destination, and he spent as much time looking in his rear-view mirror as he did at the road in front of him.

"Under the seat," he said, as we turned into one of the lovely brownstone streets that were being recovered by the urban homesteaders. "In the bag."

The gleaming new Colt .38 was in the bag, along with a dozen bullets. There was a silencer attached to the muzzle. The blond man's face flashed through me, his surprised look when I killed him.

"Put the other piece in the bag," he said. I wiped it with a handkerchief and put it in the bag. Bird was playing "April in Paris". I remembered a vagrant evening long ago, standing outside some joint on Fifty-second Street when I was fifteen, leaning on a car in the summer evening, listening to Bird. That same night I heard Tatum playing across the street, all of it free, the doors wide open because there was no air-conditioning then. Bird and Tatum and the joints of Fifty-second Street were all gone now. I put the bullets in my pocket and shoved the gun into my belt under the jacket. Jimmy pulled up in front of Small's and double-parked. We got out and went back into the bar.

"There was a call for you," the bartender said to me. "Guy say you should look at the *Daily News*. Real careful. He say you should look at page twenty-six. He say you'd understand."

He had the *Daily News* in his hand, folded back to page twenty-six. He handed it to me and walked away. Jimmy leaned in and read with me:

EX-FIGHTER
DIES IN CRASH

A forty-two-year-old ex-fighter died last night in a fiery crash on the Brooklyn-Queens Expressway.

Police said that Bernard Mullins, a onetime highly-regarded New York Golden Glover, was

alone in his 1979 Chevrolet when the car went
out of control and struck a guard rail.

    Mullins was born in Ballina, Co. Mayo,
Ireland, and came to this country . . .

I didn't bother reading the rest. I told Jimmy I'd call
him later and went out to the street. Marta's car was still
there. It was time to go to Brooklyn.

26 The terrible thing, somehow, was that the day was so
beautiful. The first warm sun of spring had arrived in
the city, and what had seemed cold and oblique in the Jersey
morning, was now full of the promise of life and renewal. I
saw a heavyset black man washing the windows of his
grocery store, and kids starting a crap game, and three
beautiful young girls walking in a sassy way past the
shuttered doors of the old Apollo Theater. I had probably sat
with their mothers in that theater, when Basie was on stage
with the greatest of all bands, or while Little Willie John did
one final gig before going to prison, or Dinah Washington
sang "Unforgettable" while the balconies throbbed and
roared. Redd Fox played there, too, before television tamed
him, and the great musicians and the rock 'n' rollers, too.
Dexter Gordon told me once that the musicians all stayed in
the hotel behind the theater on One Hundred and Twenty-
sixth Street and fought for windowed rooms because they
overlooked the dressing rooms where the chorus girls
changed. When I was a kid reporter, it was still possible to
go up to the Apollo on a Friday night and eat dinner at
Frank's and maybe stroll down to Minton's for bebop or
over to Sugar Ray's for some talk and a sight of the greatest
of all champions. The last time Sugar Ray was in New York
I told him I'd meet him uptown; Frank's was closed, and so
was the Apollo, and there were no beboppers at Minton's
and Sugar Ray's had fallen to the taxmen. He met me on the
corner of One Hundred and Twenty-fifth and Lenox. I

looked at Ray, and he looked at me and said: "Where the fuck'd everybody go?"

They'd all gone away, and now Sugar Ray lived in Los Angeles, and I was a middle-aged man, with a daughter in terrible trouble because I had played too long at the games of youth. I didn't believe in many things anymore, not the way other people did, and I was caught in a struggle with people who believed. They believed in God, in heaven, in abstractions. I had believed in God once, too, when I was very small, and afraid of the dark. Later I had believed in art and in love, and there was a time when I even believed in socialism; I believed in that sad and lovely dream right up to the moment when Pol Pot and his Cambodian allies began to murder everybody who wore eyeglasses. I still believed in Sugar Ray.

I pulled over to the curb at First Avenue and went to a row of phone booths. Two of the phones had been ripped out. The third was intact. I called Marta Torres at her office. I gave her the address of the house in Brooklyn, and told her that if she hadn't heard from me by five o'clock, she should call Charlie Kelly.

"Be careful," she said softly.

"I'll try."

The sun glittered on the East River as I drove downtown on the FDR Drive. Tugboats chugged nobly to the north, hauling fruits and vegetables to the markets of the south Bronx. I played the radio; there was still no news. On WNEW they played Bing Crosby's version of "How Are Things In Glocca Mora?" and I shut it off. That was some other Ireland: leprechauns and colleens and "Danny Boy." I hated that fraudulent Ireland: it was like the St. Patrick's Day Parade itself, with politicians wearing green ties, and bloated fatheads from the respectable Irish organizations up on reviewing stands in top hats, and drunken kids from the suburbs throwing up on their shoes in the side streets. It had nothing to do with the Ireland of Yeats and O'Casey and James Connolly; it certainly had nothing to do with men moving in the shadows of hard northern cities, their caps pulled tightly against the steady dirty rain, men prepared to die, men like Steel.

He was here.

Somewhere in the city, beyond this thick traffic, beyond those giant apartment houses, somewhere out there, Steel was carrying the diamond of his dream. As I moved past the Seventy-second Street exit, driving slowly south to the Brooklyn Bridge, I thought about Steel's ascetic face, and his questions about baseball; I had liked him, even respected him. But I knew, as I came closer to Brooklyn, that if he had set up the kidnapping of my daughter, I would probably have to kill him.

Traffic narrowed to one lane near the bridge. I could see the empty buildings of the Navy Yard, where I had worked when I was a boy, after my father had died. There were giant nineteenth-century warehouses around the base of the bridge, all of them being refurnished as condominiums now that the old jobs had departed for the South and the Orient. The sun splashed against their facades, brightening the dirty brick, and I wondered if April had ever seen those buildings and if she hadn't, whether she ever would. She was older now. I could really take her around this city now. I could show her the places and tell her the tale of the town, its history and crimes, and all its triumphs, too. I wanted to do that. Very much. I wondered how they had brought her here; by airplane, of course; and then probably to some small airfield in Jersey or New England, and then into a car, and then to this place that only Sheila Rafferty and a dead man knew about. One man's love nest is another man's safe house.

The traffic moved more swiftly. I went up onto the great bridge, with the harbor spread out to my right. The steel cables were humming in the spring breeze. I looked in the rearview mirror again. Nobody was following me. I was sure of that.

Then I was in Brooklyn.

I left the car along the edge of Prospect Park at First Street, climbing up over a bench into the dense trees. Then I walked through the trees until I was facing Carroll Street.

The street sloped away to the harbor, and the day was so clear I could see the Statue of Liberty and Staten Island, and the polluted smear of New Jersey beyond. Traffic was sparse. I looked down the street at the houses. There were brownstones on both sides of Carroll Street, and maple trees emerging from winter and cars parked tightly from one end to the other. A sanitation truck was at the bottom of the street, blocking traffic, slowly working its way up to the parkside. I knew that the even numbers were on the right side of the street, so I left the park and walked across the wide avenue to the corner, to see the numbers on the far side of the street. Three houses down from the corner was 431. I knew that 432 had to be directly across the street.

I thought about my options. Frontal assault was idiotic; those brownstone houses are entered through iron gates under the stoop, or sets of double doors at the top of the stairs. All of them had trapdoors on the rooftops, leading into the attics. But I'd have to go through another house to get to the rooftop of 432, and that meant using the gun, or risking being reported as a burglar from the houses across the street. That would bring cops. I didn't want cops. I was also certain that Jack McDaid would have sealed the entrances from the roof. There was probably a fire escape down the back of the house, but McDaid probably had barred the back windows, too.

I returned to the trees, and watched the sanitation truck coming up the block. If I called the cops, or worse, the FBI, they'd probably shoot their way in. I just couldn't take that chance; I'd covered too many of those stories, with the blood on the floor when it was over.

Then I saw Sheila Rafferty.

She was getting out of a car behind the sanitation truck. The car was double-parked. And she was going behind the car to open the trunk.

I came out of the park in a hurry, using the sanitation truck to block her view of me.

I crossed the avenue, and went down the street, and reached her as she started to heft two bags of groceries from the trunk.

141

"Need some help, lady?" I said.

She made a small "oh" sound and glanced at the garbagemen and then at 432 and started to drop one of the grocery bags.

"I have a gun in this pocket," I said. "It's loaded. I'll blow a fuckin' hole right through you if you don't do what I tell you to do. Got it?" She nodded. "Now you're gonna smile at me, and you're gonna hand me one of those bags. Just like we were old friends from the neighborhood. Then you're gonna walk into the house, and you're not gonna say a word, because if you do I'll put a couple of holes in you."

She smiled and handed me a bag of groceries.

"I wish you understood, Sam," she said, the smile pasted on her face.

"I understand perfectly," I said. "You don't deserve to live in this world."

We were in the areaway. The sanitation truck rumbled around the corner out of sight. She fumbled in her jeans pockets and came out with a ring of keys that would have ruptured a janitor. One of them fit the black iron gate. We went into the sour-smelling space beneath the stoop. There was another key for the door leading to the vestibule. She found it with the familiarity of someone who had been to this house many times.

She opened the door.

An albino man was standing there, his skin as white as his hair, his eyes pink. I shoved the gun into his belly.

"Don't say a fuckin' word," I said, handing him the grocery bag and then taking a gun off his belt. I took the keys from Sheila, slipped them into my pocket, and nodded for them to walk ahead of me. We went down the hall, past a flight of stairs that led to the upper floors and a set of closed oaken sliding doors to the kitchen in the back. The house had a sour indoor smell to it, as if it had been a long time since a window had been opened. Sweat, beer, cooking smells had melded together, along with some damp rotting odor that could have come from a backed-up sewer. The albino had the smell on him, too, as if he had been infected by the house. There was a door at the end of the hall. I motioned for them to stop.

I started to open the door.

Sheila dropped her groceries, the door was jerked open, and I was staring at an M-16.

The man holding it was Manning.

"Come in, Mister Briscoe," he said.

The albino took my guns. I stepped into the kitchen. There was a round oak table, some chairs, a fridge, a door leading to the backyard, another to a bathroom and double doors leading to the dining room. Manning handled the M-16 like a man who wanted to use it.

"We saw you from the time you crossed the street the first time," he said. "Do you think we're fools?"

"Yeah," I said. "This is lunacy. You'll all get caught or killed."

"We don't think so," Manning said. I looked at Sheila Rafferty. She was leaning against the sink, lighting a cigarette. There was a serene, almost blissful look on her face.

"You were in this from the beginning, I guess?" I said to her.

"Of course," she said. "You Irish jerks will believe anything."

"Yeah, particularly while we're fucking," I said. Manning glanced at her in a hard way. "When you were fucking Jack McDaid did you think of the Lord? Did you think of Christ the Leader? Was it the ultimate sacrifice? Did you expect to get the Mary Magdalene Award when you went to heaven?" I laughed drily. "And what was on your mind when you were fucking me? And crying in my arms?"

"Shut up, Briscoe," Manning said.

"No, seriously, I just want to know," I said. "You people must have worked on this for months." I sat down at the round table, keeping my hands in front of me so they wouldn't get trigger nutty. The albino leaned against the closed double doors.

"Let me tell you what I think you did," I said. "I think Sheila here has been involved with you whackos for years. I think all that stuff you told me, Sheila, about your father and drugs and the rest of it—the early part of your life—that was true, wasn't it?" She shrugged in agreement. "But from there you didn't go to any commune, or get tied up with the Irish nationalists. You found Jesus. Lots of people your age did the same thing. The amphetamine road to salvation. You were probably hooked up with this asshole, Machine Gun Manning."

"He's my husband," she said.

I laughed out loud. "Well, I'll be damned."

"We didn't ask you for any talk, Briscoe," Manning said.

"Oh, it doesn't matter, Robert," Sheila said, her sense of command bending him into silence. "Let him rave. We've got—" She glanced at her watch. "Four hours to go."

"Thanks, baby," I said. "So that made it even more logical. The Church, run by the old lunatic and his son, the degenerate, are hooked up with the hard-liners in Belfast. The old man doesn't know shit from shinola about anything anymore, even crossing the street. So he wasn't much involved. But Junior was. Junior likes money. So you get offered a deal. Or Junior gets offered a deal. In one master stroke, the IRA could be crippled for years and totally disgraced."

Manning's face was twitching now. He looked disapprovingly at Sheila, who was cool and quiet, smoking a Viceroy, with a thin smile on her face. It was as if some new information was eating away at him, and it was all about her.

"So you set up this scheme," I said. "You would blow up the ballroom of the Plaza Hotel, killing the four top Irish-American politicians, and whoever else hadn't succumbed to the rubber chicken dinner. Sheila here, who had been planted months ago with Jack McDaid to spy on the Irish over here, would also work with Jack McDaid to set up a giant arms deal. The deal would be so big it would empty the IRA treasury, but might make a general uprising a reality. Poor Steel was certain it was legitimate, because his people had always trusted Jack McDaid. So he scrambled around and raised the money, probably with some bank robberies over there. And when it came time for the final payment, he made me the courier. A cashier's check, probably. From a Swiss bank. Or Barclay's. One phony corporation to another."

Sheila had an admiring look on her face. Manning didn't like it. I kept talking. As long as I was talking, I was breathing.

"Your people suspected me from the moment I arrived in Belfast, figured that after seeing Steel, I was carrying the money; they were ordered to follow me. Being morons, they went too far, searching my room in Geneva, tearing up my article, chasing me around an Alp. But they did find out where my daughter went to school. That was helpful. That could be an ace in the hole. You were glad about that. My uncle Frank's death had nothing to do with any of this. He just got it because of his entire life."

Manning's eyes kept moving from me to Sheila. He didn't like what he saw on her face. The albino seemed in a trance. He never moved from the sliding double doors.

"So I made it home, and delivered the money," I said. "Your, uh, husband here was told to come over to the bar at closing time. You'd seen so little of him, while fucking Jack McDaid, that you even had to give him directions. You also warned him about me. The asshole even followed me, to make sure I left Queens, but I screwed things up by kicking his ass. Meanwhile, little you, Sheila, were inside with Jack. You told him to give you the check and meet you at his car. Something like that. And on the way out you set the timer on the bomb. Thirty seconds? A minute? The bartenders took too much time saying goodnight on the sidewalk and the bomb went off a little early."

She smiled. "And so I was rescued by big brave you," she said. "My Lochinvar."

"Yeah," I said. "You were shook up, though. And you had to play the role. You went home with me." I turned to Manning. "Great tits on this dame."

"Let me—"

"Oh, Robert, grow up!" Sheila said. The albino seemed to be blushing.

"Anyway," I said, "you now had a ton of money to deliver to Junior Parsons. His bankers would never question a check from him. It was, after all, a good check. And Junior must have been grateful. After all, look what you'd done. But it still wasn't enough. You wanted to get Steel, too. You had to get him here somehow, away from the protection of the Belfast Command, so you, or Barney Mullins, contacted him. Barney, the dumb shit, probably still thought he was fighting for his country. Steel agreed to come. Probably through Canada. When Barney Mullins got suspicious, you knocked him off."

"I don't want to hear anymore of this," Manning said. He fondled the M-16, looked jittery, then waited for his wife to answer him.

"He's better than television," she said. "We have nothing to do for awhile." She looked at me. "He's a writer. Let him write with his mouth."

"I was more than a writer to you, wasn't I, baby?" I said. "Like Junior was more than a preacher. You know, I start to understand even more of this thing. You find Jesus. You join the Church of Christ the Leader. It's great. It's true. You believe. You meet Manning. He believes. He's a fine southern gentleman. You marry him. But you also meet Junior Parsons. Now as a writer, I have to wonder. Was it possible that before you ever got to Jack McDaid, before you got to me, you also found redemption in the arms of Junior Parsons? My goodness, could that be? Could you have also been fucking a son of God? Could you have been the duty piece of ass for the whitehaired one? And if so, is it possible that this had nothing to do with God at all? Or that—"

Manning lowered the gun to fire, and Sheila lunged at him, deflecting the barrel. I didn't wait. I leaped from the chair, slammed them both against the albino, grabbed the M-16 and chopped at Manning's skull. I whirled and kicked the albino in the balls, and then hit Sheila with the hardest right hand I'd thrown in years. She crumpled and fell, with blood pouring from her nose. The albino moaned. I put the M-16 on the table and hit him over the head with a chair.

It was very quiet then.

I took the pistols out of the albino's pockets and lugged him into the bathroom, dumping him in the tub. I found a length of clothesline in the pantry, cut off two pieces with a bread knife, tied his hands and feet, and shoved a washcloth in his mouth. I did the same with Manning. There were no washcloths left by the time I got to Sheila. I tore off her blouse and shoved it in her mouth. The jaw was unhinged.

I cracked open the door to the hall. If April were upstairs, there might be another man guarding her. The hall was quiet, and I heard nothing from upstairs. I knew I would have to go room to room, and decided to take the M-16 with me. It felt strange in my hands; I hadn't seen one since the fall of Saigon.

I started with the closed double doors. I opened them slowly, waited, heard nothing. But a stench flowed out. I opened the door wider. In the long dark room, I could see the shapes of stuffy Victorian furniture, a broken porcelain clock on a mantel over a sealed fireplace, and an unmade bed on the right, placed clumsily against the wall. At the far end of the room, on a couch next to the windows, I could see a man lying facedown. I didn't have to take his pulse to know that he was dead. And I didn't need to hold his face in my hands to know who he was. It was Steel. There was a hole behind his right ear.

I backed out of the room.

27 I wanted to take that M-16 and go into the bathroom and destroy the people who were piled in there. I wanted to spread death around. There had been so much of it now: Frank, Jack McDaid, the blond guy in Jersey, Barney Mullins, and now Steel. I could just spread it around a little more. Just shoot everyone concerned into small

pieces. It didn't matter now, Sheila had said. It didn't. She
knew. She had blood all over her. They all did. So did I.

But I didn't do anything with the M-16.

I went up the stairs, trying each room, as quietly as
possible. There was a musty unused smell to this part of the
house, but it was a lot nicer than the smell of death on the
first floor. I found a locked door on the top floor. I kicked it
off its hinges.

April was lying on the bed, her hands and legs tied to
bedposts, and a tee shirt in her mouth. Her eyes were wide
in alarm. I removed the tee shirt.

"Oh, Daddy," she said. "Daddy, Daddy, Daddy."

We drove out of Brooklyn in the early darkness. I was
through with guns now. They were in a pile in the house
we'd left behind. The skyline seemed immense, rising
before us out of the black harbor. April talked almost
clinically about what had happened to her—the kidnapping,
and a black van, and then an airplane. It made two stops
before the final one. The first stop was in a place that was
very hot; she thought it must have been in Africa, and I
agreed. The men took their masks off after that stop. One of
them was large and burly, she said, with a red moustache.
That was Redmond. The other was pale and slight, almost
an albino. They were in a small plane. The door to the
pilot's cabin was sealed. The men had guns. They almost
never talked. She grew weary and slept. They blindfolded
her when they made the second stop. The door opened and
closed, and it was very cold. It might have been Canada.
She wasn't certain. There was a third and final stop, and she
was blindfolded again, and bound, and placed in another
van. She had woken up in this room. The albino brought her
food and then left. A redhaired woman also came up to see
her. She never saw the moustached man again. But she
remembered the woman.

"She asked me all sorts of strange questions," April
said, as we came off the bridge and went across Chambers
Street to the West Side. "She wanted to know about you.
But she also wanted to know if I believed in God and

whether you believed in God, and did you ever try to teach me to be a good Christian. Do you know her?"

"I did."

"Is she crazy?"

"She might be," I said. "But she wasn't alone."

"Oh, my."

We stopped for a red light at the corner of West Street before making the long run uptown. A giant semi came roaring along the cobblestones, making lights. Ours turned green. The truck kept coming, ran the red light, and then backfired. April broke. She jumped, she sobbed; she bawled like a baby. I turned the corner slowly, and stopped, and put my arms around her and hugged her until she stopped crying and fell asleep. I put her head on my lap and drove uptown. She was learning very quickly that the world was a strange and dangerous place.

I woke her up when we stopped in front of the marquee of the Mayflower. Her eyes moved in a hunted way, as she watched me slip a bellboy five bucks to park the car, and then pick up my key at the front desk.

"Miss Torres is already upstairs," the night clerk said. He smiled and so did I. April held my hand as we went into the elevator. I looked at my watch and at the clock in the lobby. It was a quarter to seven.

"Thank God," Marta said, after we let ourselves in. I introduced her to April, and they smiled at each other in a careful way. Marta took her into the bathroom, and ran a bath, while I ordered her a hamburger from room service. I sat back in an easy chair, and had never felt more tired. I closed my eyes, thinking: it's over. I've got my daughter back. She's alive. She's safe. Other people are dead, but my daughter is safe. That's it. The game's over.

But I knew it wasn't over.

There was one more believer to find. He had beautiful white hair and a lovely voice, and he was the engine of all the killing.

I had to see Parsons.

I picked up the phone and called Charlie Kelly. They

were waiting for my call and told me to hold on. I held on for a long time. April came out of the bathroom in a white hotel bathrobe. Her face was drawn, she needed sleep, but she was alive. Marta was another matter; she stared at me in a brutal way.

"That better be room service," she said.

"The food's on the way," I said.

Then Charlie came on, his voice crackling from a radio phone. I waved the women into the bedroom, and then quickly told Charlie what had happened in Brooklyn. I didn't tell him about New Jersey. He said he would have some men in Carroll Street right away. I suggested he send the FBI over to the Mayflower in the morning, and April could tell them what had happened. He listened, grunted, listened some more. He was not happy.

"You might as well get your ass over here," he said.

"Where?"

"The Plaza. The Bomb Squad went through the joint and found nothing. The Secret Service didn't want to hear anything except call the dinner off. Me, too. Get them the fuck out of there, is my suggestion. But it's the goddamned politicians themselves. They say they don't believe it. So they went ahead. Now they're all in there, and we're still searching the place."

"What's your instinct?"

"You know that bum Barney Mullins? I found out twenty minutes ago, he worked in the Plaza for eleven years. That's why they recruited him. He was an electrician. He knew every crevice, every crack, every air-conditioning duct in the joint. My instinct? I think there's stuff in there. I think there's someone around with a transmitter who can push a button and blow the thing from here to Pennsylvania. With everybody in it."

"So why don't you evacuate the joint?"

"Simple," he said. "The pols are inside already. So are a couple of thousand other people. There's no way to empty the joint without letting the world know. The guy with the button would just press it, and that's all she wrote."

"So what are you doing?"

"Looking for the guy with the button."

28 In the mauve evening light, the Plaza rose from its broad open square like an antique dream. Limousines and taxis pulled up to the main entrance in a steady flow, discharging gowned and tuxedoed passengers. A lone police car was parked beside the entrance to Central Park, which spread away in brooding darkness to the north. And behind a barrier of gray wooden horses several hundred pickets chanted the old slogans—"England Out of Ireland" and "Free the North"—to the general indifference of passing New Yorkers. Horse-drawn cabs waited at the curb for their nightly cargo of tourists, conventioneers and lovers, ignoring the demonstration. Pretty girls sat with their young men along the rim of the dry fountain. I hurried past them to Fifth Avenue. Charlie Kelly waited for me under the marquee of the Sherry-Netherland Hotel, across the square from the Plaza.

"Well?" I said.

"You're in a real fuckin' mess this time, Sam."

"It'll be a worse mess if this guy pushes that button," I said. "Wherever the hell he is."

"I've got guys going floor to floor in every building around here, taking a look. But suppose he's not here? Suppose he goes by in a car or a van? Suppose he's got some asshole out there at that demo?"

"He'd like that," I said. "He'd like the irony."

"So what do I do? Lock up all two hundred fifty of them? Besides, as soon as we start to lock them up, he pushes the button."

I asked him about the range of an electronic device. He shrugged. A couple of blocks.

"Look at these office buildings around here," he said. "The guy could be in any one of them." He looked at his watch: seven-forty-five. "He could be squirreled away in some dentist's office, some advertising company, who knows? He doesn't even have to be watching the office

151

when he blows it up. He can just press a button, roll over, and go to sleep."

"What can we do out here, Charlie?"

"Watch it blow."

I exhaled. He lit a cigar. He told me he was going over to the General Motors Building. He had a car down on Madison Avenue and plainclothes men all over the place.

"If it blows up," he said, "I'll see you in Clarke's."

"Yeah," I said. "I'll call that biology teacher."

"Or an ambulance."

He walked away. I stood on the corner of Fifth Avenue, feeling hopeless, my eyes drawn to the Plaza. And then, on the other side of the street, I saw a young bony Irishman walking quickly across Fifth Avenue into Fifty-eighth Street. He was wearing dark glasses, and once he looked over his shoulder at the Plaza. Just once. And I knew him. It was the young Irish kid who had done such a terrible job of guarding me in the Gramercy Gym.

I hurried across the street after him, dodging taxis.

"Hey, you!" I shouted. "Hey, Sandy!"

He turned, saw me, took his hands out of his pockets and hesitated. I thumped the heel of my left hand against his shoulder and hit him a crippling, short right hand under the heart. He stopped dead in pain. The glasses fell off; his eyes were still swollen and full of hurt. I lifted him under the arms and bounced him against the wall, as if I were holding up a drunk. He shuddered. Two business types got out of a cab, gave us a blank look, then went into the Playboy Club. Nobody else noticed.

"Sandy, I have to give this to you fast," I said. "Everybody's been caught: Sheila and the others. Steel is dead. Barney is dead. But the Plaza Hotel is full of people who don't have to be dead."

"Up the IRA!" he whispered. "Up Provos!"

"You were set up, boy," I said. "Sheila was working for the other side. They set this job up to discredit the Provos. Now, if you really want to help the cause, tell me where you helped Barney install the triggering device."

"Steel dead?" he said. "I don't believe you."

"If we had time," I said, "I'd take you out to Brooklyn and show you the body. But we don't have that kind of time."

He studied me, his eyes wet. He started to say something, checked himself. The world must have seemed a terrifying complex place to him in that moment. He tried to reassemble his face, a boy trying hard to look like a man. He couldn't do it.

"Right, then," he said. "I'll tell you."

I left Sandy to his pain and his misery and walked into the small lobby of the Sherry-Netherland. I knew the desk clerk, but he was very nervous. I told him I had to meet Charlie Kelly upstairs. He said Charlie wasn't there. Yes, I said, but there were other cops here, weren't there? He nodded discreetly. I'm helping them, I said. Trust me. He nodded again and then let me go to the elevator. I told the young operator to take me to the top floor.

I got off and waited for him to leave. The hall was very quiet. All the doors were closed, and I walked down the corridor, looking for the door to a workroom that Sandy said was cut through damask wallpaper into the wall. I almost missed it. There was a tiny handle, recessed into the door.

I turned the handle slowly, afraid of a squeak. It turned. And then I jerked it open violently.

Junior Parsons stood there, at the end of an eight-foot deep room, his face alarmed. His hands were empty. We both froze. Through the window behind him, I could see the Plaza, and part of the roof of the Sherry-Netherland, with an iron stairway leading up to a higher part of the roof. The room was jammed with shelves full of janitorial supplies, mops, brooms, two vacuum cleaners. On a small table, I could see a pack of Merits, a pistol, a set of binoculars, and a black metallic box the size of a tape recorder.

"Don't even try," I said.

He smiled in an oily way. "Try what?"

I stepped closer. We were three or four feet apart.

"It's all over, Junior," I said. "You're the last one on

the loose. The cops have everybody who's alive. The morgue is picking up the dead. Don't be dumb."

"I'm just up here looking at the heavens."

"Yeah. With a big cashier's check from Barclay's Bank in your pocket."

He blinked. "What does that mean?"

"It means you're either a racket guy or a nut," I said. "Or maybe both. The racket guy grabbed a lot of money from the IRA. The nut is about to kill a lot of people, and blame the IRA. It's all God's work, I guess. Isn't it, Junior?"

"You must be Briscoe."

"That's right," I said. "Still busting balls."

"If you try to do something to me," he said coldly, "someone you love will be hurt."

"I'm afraid not," I said. "My daughter's a hell of a lot safer now than you are."

For the first time, he seemed afraid.

"I might not be much of a father," I said, "but if you fuck with my family, I'll wreck you. And it's gonna be fun wrecking you. You're gonna have a real good time walking around without kneecaps. Ever see a guy without knees try to ski? Or cross a street? It starts to hurt the brain. You'll end up a babbling moron like your father."

"What about my father?" he said, eyes alarmed, hard highlights burning in the irises. "What have you done to my father?"

"Oh, he's alive. His body is alive. The brain is in an advanced state of decomposition. He's babbling away about Franco and Eleanor Roosevelt and God. The poor fucking lunatic apparently believes all that." I smiled. "You never bought any of it, did you, Junior? You were just another hustler in the God racket, weren't you?"

He looked at me for a long moment. Then: "No."

"So how'd you get this tangled up? How'd you end up sitting in this room, about to blow a lot of people to kingdom come?"

He sighed and leaned back against a broom closet. His

eyes never even went to the table or the little metal box. He was a superb actor.

"It wasn't easy being his son," he said. "I didn't want it. They made me do it. It was like . . . like the family business. I tried to break away. I tried what I could."

"That means you wanted to get laid, I guess."

He sniffed. "I tried to get out of it. I thought I could be an actor. Can you believe it? In California when I was young, everybody thought he could be a movie star. Even me. But I didn't have it. I tried. But I didn't have whatever it is that they have."

"Heart?"

"That's easy for you to say," he blurted. "You don't know anything about me. You don't know anything about how I suffered. About the women I loved and could never have. What do you know? You're a newspaperman."

"Was Sheila Rafferty one of those women?" I said.

His eyes skittered. "She's married to one of our people."

"So what?"

He shook his head slowly. "Maybe she was."

Manning and I were both right.

"So what are you doing here without her?"

"This is *business*."

"God's business?"

"Yes!"

"Bullshit. You're here because you made a deal. And you're surrounded by such a bunch of retarded jerks you could never trust them to pull it off. You had to do it yourself. You made a deal with people on the other side and they paid you a lot of money. What was the fee? The gun money you could rip off from the IRA? Was that it? Or was it even more? Maybe a nice neat check stashed in a numbered account somewhere. You could get out of the God racket for good. You could grab a million from the Church while the old man nodded, and maybe another million here, and you could get out of it altogether. Take Sheila Rafferty and your lifetime supply of alligator shoes and go to Switzerland or Brazil. Get new names and new passports. That is not hard if you have the money."

I was talking faster now. As long as I was talking, he couldn't reach for that button or the pistol.

"What if I did want something like that?" he said. "What's wrong with that? My father swore that I would never get a dime from him, no matter how much I repented. I had a job. That's all. On a salary. Even though I brought in the money. That's how he punished me. So what's wrong with what I'm doing? What's wrong with it?"

"What's wrong? Think about it, schmuck."

He glanced out the window, then at me, and then he lunged for the box. I pulled him back by the collar, twisted him around in the narrow space, dug my thumbs into his neck, and put myself between him and the box.

"You little cocksucker," I said. "I oughtta break your fuckin' neck."

I didn't. He brought his knee up between my legs, driving pain through me. I released his neck and fell back against the table and, feeling something break under my weight, I spun awkwardly, catching the triggering device before it hit the floor. I hit the floor myself, holding the box tight to my chest, trying to see where the gun had gone.

Junior began stomping me, his beautiful white hair bouncing like a halo around his ferocious face. I saw the gun, and grabbed for it. He kicked me in the shoulder, and then in the chest, just missing the black box. When I rolled away from the kicks, he went for the gun.

With one hand I pushed the black box out to the carpeted hall. He grabbed the gun, and I clenched his wrist. The gun was aimed at the wall, and I dug my thumb into his wrist. He fired, a bullet caroming around the small room. Then another, puncturing a can of lubricant. He pulled back, breaking my grip, and I rolled to the hall as he fired twice more, the bullets phwocking into the wall. Doors opened all along the corridor, but when startled guests saw me flattened against the wall beside the workroom, they slammed their doors shut behind them. Now I knew they'd be calling the front desk, and the cops would assemble here from other parts of the hotel, but I wasn't going to wait.

I listened, heard his feet on metal, then a door slam, thinking: he's gone to the roof.

I picked up the black box and carried it like a tray of eggs about thirty feet down the hall. I left it lying in the middle of the carpet—a gift for Charlie Kelly. Then I went to the workroom again. I wanted Junior Parsons for myself.

The room was empty, the thick motor oil dripping slowly to the floor. On the floor were the binoculars, the pack of Merits, about a dozen cigarette butts. And a wallet. An expensive Dunhill wallet. I picked it up and looked at the contents in the light from the hall. The usual things—driver's license, business cards, every credit card known to man, membership in various religious organizations, most of them connected to broadcasting. And folded inside, very crisply, was a check. It was a cashier's check from Credit Suisse for five hundred thousand dollars. I tucked the check into my back pocket, dropped the wallet on the floor, and stepped outside to the iron stairs leading to the roof.

"Parsons!"

My voice was snatched by the whining wind and thrown into the night. There were pebbles and tar paper under my feet, and three terraces, a brick-enclosed water tower hovering above everything. The tower looked like some clumsily designed device for exploring distant planets, waiting only a signal to be launched. Its bulk made the roof even darker. A low barricade ran around the edge of the roof, and drainpipes led into sculpted gargoyles. Beyond the edge of the roof I could see the Plaza, standing above its now tiny square.

"The cops are everywhere, Parsons," I shouted into the darkness. "Don't be a jerk!"

He had a gun and I didn't. He had studied the terrain of the roof in the daylight, and I hadn't. Reason said: leave him to the cops. But something more than reason was moving through me: Parsons was at the heart of everything that had happened. His greed was part of it, the terrible American need for more. But there was also the crazy megalomania that came from growing up with a lunatic father, sick with certainty and belief; Junior had once embraced doubt, and then rejected it for the God racket, and went on to license the death of others. He had made his deal with the religious nuts of Northern Ireland, a deal for one final score: financial, political, personal. There was Sheila, too. Maybe more than anything else. She was beautiful. She was smart and tough. Most of all, she was young. With her, he could have the life he had missed. I tried to pity him, but the feeling would not come. I thought about my daughter being slapped around by grown men, and bundled into airplanes. I thought about Steel's blank ascetic face as he lay in the stink of his released bowels in that room in Brooklyn, his death a victory for the bleak northern god of denial and punishment. I thought of poor Barney Mullins, with his dot of lost courage, dying in flames on a highway far from the roads of his birth. I thought about Jack McDaid's permanent romanticism, his dream of Ireland pulling him into a treasonous bed, his wife's ruined voice on the phone and the lies she would have to tell her children for the rest of their lives. I thought about that poor blond kid, nameless and without history to the man who killed him: me. The Parsons stain was on me, and on all the others who had been touched by him. Even Sandy, the saddest of all, dumb and tentative and half-formed, a boy prepared to die for Ireland, but as scared as all boys have ever been; he would live from this night on with the belief that he was an informer, and that he had informed because of fear.

I stood up and shouted: "Parsons!"

He fired from somewhere above me, the bullet chipping stone and whining away toward the park. I went flat behind the ledge, and crawled on my belly to the right. From above, he couldn't see me clearly, but I couldn't see him at all.

He fired again, the bullet pinging against stone, and then rattling into one of the bronze drainpipes. I counted: six shots. I heard the clicking gun. Then the sound of the useless gun clattering on brick. Now I could take him. Now I could hurt him. Just a little. Just enough to make him feel some pain. After that, the cops would have him, and there would be a trial, and he would hire brilliant lawyers, and there would be talk of the privileges of a clergyman, and his father would be put on television, with a ventriloquist doing the talking, to appeal for funds. The money would roll in from all the suckers, from those who remembered the old man when he was young, and from all the new ones, all the believers in conspiracies and certainties. Junior Parsons would become a martyr in his cell, and politicians who convicted blacks and Latins in the press before trial would reserve judgment until later. Manning and Sheila and the albino would go on trial separately, and Parsons would stand above everything, talking of God. That would all be later. I wanted to hurt him first.

I stood up.

And he crashed into me, hitting me with his wiry tennis player's body, knocking me over. I turned and he smashed me with his fist along the side of my head. He got up and tried again to stomp me. But I grabbed his foot with both hands, pulled him off balance, stood up, and swung him as if he were a sack. He slammed into the leg of the water tower. He lay there, stunned, and I stood over him, breathless. Suddenly he kicked me in the chest. I teetered, wondering where the edge of the roof was. And then he came at me in a charge. I stopped him with a hook, then drove a punch deep into his stomach. He bent over, sick and hurt. I stepped back to let him fall. He didn't.

"You . . . bastard," he said.

He drew on some final terrible reserve, and charged.

I swung at him out of my own exhaustion. And missed.

He lurched past me out of my sight and over the edge.

Just like that.

In silence.

Gone.

I stepped over to the edge, afraid to look, afraid of dizziness and nausea and falling. And saw Parsons beneath me.

He was holding on to a green rim of copper drainpiping

about two feet below the edge. Fifth Avenue was below him. It looked as far away as the moon.

"Please . . ." he whispered hoarsely.

His face contorted with the effort to hold on.

"Help . . . me."

If he let go with one hand to grab mine, he'd be gone.

"I want to live," he stuttered. "God forgive me . . . I want to . . . live."

I reached down instinctively, and trying to save the man's life, I grabbed him by his beautiful white hair.

It peeled off in my hand.

The doomed astonished eyes widened in the bald head, his mouth opened to scream. And then Martin Parsons Junior, messenger of God, fell into the endlessly empty night air.

I didn't move. I didn't watch. I looked up at the March moon, and then at the toupee in my hand, and then, wildly, hysterically, without control or thought, my body shaking, I began to laugh.

29 When I opened the door to the suite at the Mayflower, there were five large suitcases blocking the passage. For a moment, I thought I'd opened the wrong door. That would have been no surprise; for ten days I'd been opening the wrong doors everywhere. Then down the narrow hall in the living room, I saw Elaine. She was perfectly dressed, her hair perfectly groomed, and she was perfectly located in an easy chair beside the fireplace, talking across a cocktail table at Marta. They looked up in a startled way, as if they had been talking about me.

"Why, Sam," Elaine said, standing up and rushing to me. She put her arms around me and held me tight. Marta moved to the window, her back to us, and gazed out at Central Park. I felt myself tense, but Elaine broke the moment and stepped away. "I'm sorry I was so terrible to you on the phone, Sam."

"Forget it. It was a million years ago."

"I was just so upset, Sam," she said. "And now everything's all right, isn't it?"

"I hope," I said.

"And April will be all right?"

"Well, she told me a few weeks ago she wanted to be a writer," I said. "Now she's got something to write about."

She snorted. "With any luck, *that* won't happen."

"With any luck," I repeated dully.

I eased away from her and went over to Marta. I never knew a woman who was comfortable in the presence of her lover's ex-wife; Marta was no exception, but she was giving it her best shot.

"Well, I guess I can go home now," she said brightly. I could hear Elaine opening the straps of a suitcase.

"Please don't," I said.

"You guys probably have a lot to talk about."

"Less than you think."

Room service was closed, but the Carnegie Deli was always open. Marta wanted only coffee. She smiled at me, and turned to Elaine.

"Are you hungry, Elaine? We're going to order some food at the Carnegie."

"No, thank you, dear," Elaine said, too sweetly. "I'm watching my weight."

That "dear" cost Elaine whatever goodwill Marta was carrying around with her. Marta threw me a look that said: how did you ever marry this dame in the first place? I had no look to throw back, and no convincing answer; when it's all over, there's never any way to explain. I went into the bathroom and let the water run. I took off my clothes and brushed my teeth with Marta's toothbrush, and waited until I was sure she was finished calling the Carnegie. Then I picked up the bathroom extension, got an outside line, and dialed Small's Paradise, while slipping into the tub. A waiter told me to hold on. In the background I heard the pounding commotion of a great bar band. Then: "Yeah?"

"Jimmy, it's Sam."

"Yeah," he said again, more dubiously.

"You've gotta come downtown."

"Oh, man, come *on*," he said. "It's almost midnight. There's a woman at the bar could give me cardiac arrest just holdin' my hand, and you—"

"There's an envelope at the desk of the Mayflower Hotel, on Central Park West and Sixtieth Street," I said. "I'm with my daughter now and she's fine. Everything's okay with her. But that fella I met through you, and the deal we discussed, well, it's on, as far as I'm concerned. And the envelope he was expecting is in the name of a bird. Hurry, baby. Our man might lose his patience."

"Ah, shit," Jimmy said hopelessly.

"Well, it's round trip," I said. "No reason why you can't take the lady."

"I wouldn't live past Eighty-sixth Street," he said, and hung up.

That was the end of all that. The check from the Credit Suisse was in an envelope marked Charles Parker. Jimmy would pick it up and take it to Walker Smith uptown, and then Walker Smith would decide whether he wanted to go ahead. He probably would. The guns would leave. If they made it to Ireland, they would probably cause more death, but there was nothing else I could do. This was for Steel. The cops and the morgue attendants had everybody now except Redmond, and Charlie Kelly had told me about Redmond; he had taken an afternoon plane to Montreal; he was probably on his way to England, and would certainly never be back. There was nothing else to do, except mop up the blood. But those guns belonged to Steel. He had paid for them with his life. He said to me that time that he was just a soldier, one of many. The many would get what Steel had paid for.

I dried myself and dressed in my dirty clothes. The food was waiting when I came out of the bathroom. Cheese blintzes with sour cream. Cel-Ray soda. Black coffee. Marta was more relaxed now. But Elaine shifted and moved in her seat, glaring at the bedroom.

"Can't I just wake her up for a few minutes?" she said.

"Don't be ridiculous."

"Just so she knows that I'm here. That I'm all right."

"Jesus Christ, Elaine. The kid's exhausted."

"I know, but . . ."

"I told her you were okay, you were coming to New York. She knows that. You'll see her. Don't worry."

"She's my daughter, Sam."

"Mine, too!"

Marta got up. She shook her head and said, "See you two."

I stopped eating, stood up, grabbed a sip of coffee, and then went to the closet. I helped Marta on with her coat.

"Where are you two going?" Elaine said.

I tossed her the room key.

"Home," I said, taking Marta's hand. "Home."